the
originals

the
originals

cat patrick

LITTLE, BROWN AND COMPANY
NEW YORK   BOSTON

ALSO BY CAT PATRICK

Forgotten
Revived

::

Little, Brown and Company

Hachette Book Group
237 Park Avenue, New York, NY 10017
Visit our website at www.lb-teens.com

Little, Brown and Company is a division of Hachette Book Group, Inc.
The Little, Brown name and logo are trademarks of Hachette Book Group, Inc.

The publisher is not responsible for websites (or their content) that are not owned by the publisher.

First Edition: May 2013

Library of Congress Cataloging-in-Publication Data

Patrick, Cat.
The Originals / Cat Patrick. — 1st ed.
     p. cm.
   Summary: Seventeen-year-olds Lizzie, Ella, and Betsey Best are clones, raised as identical triplets by their surrogate mother but living as her one daughter, Elizabeth, until their separate abilities and a romantic relationship force a change.
   ISBN 978-0-316-21943-3
   [1. Individuality—Fiction.   2. Sisters—Fiction.   3. Single-parent families—Fiction.   4. Cloning—Fiction.   5. Dating (Social customs)—Fiction.]   I. Title.
   PZ7.P2746Ori 2013
   [Fic]—dc23

                                                            2012029853

10 9 8 7 6 5 4 3 2 1

RRD-C

Printed in the United States of America

For Erin

Mom *always said,* "Don't fight.
You'll *be best friends someday."*
Mom's *a genius.*

one

My part is first half.

I go to student government, chemistry, trigonometry, psychology, and history at school, then do the rest of the day at home. I maintain that Mom was in a mood when she made assignments this year—math and science are definitely not my best subjects. When I reminded her of this, she said, "That's exactly why you're doing first half."

I finish applying lip balm, take a step back from the sink, and frown. I'm used to looking exactly like two other people, but I'll never be used to Ella's fashion sense. I'm actually wearing an argyle cardigan.

"What's up, Ann Taylor Loft?" I mutter to myself, shaking my head.

I lean back and crane my neck so I can see the digital clock on my nightstand: It reads 6:47—thirteen minutes before I need to leave for school. One of Mom's major concerns is us standing out—and therefore being found out. So things like tardiness, bad grades, and attention-grabbing clothes are basically off-limits in the Best household.

I haven't eaten breakfast, but I don't smell bacon, so I decide to grab something from the cafeteria. Instead of sustenance, I opt for straightening. I plug in my flat iron, wait for it to heat up, then quickly but meticulously comb sections and pull the iron along, making the curls disappear. It's got its drawbacks, but at least first half means that I pick the hairstyle for the day.

Expertly moving through the darkened bedroom, I smooth down one last wrinkle at the foot of the bed and throw my pajama bottoms in the hamper. Mom tries to act mellow, but I saw her OCD forehead vein pop out yesterday when she saw the state of my room—she's got enough going on, so I cleaned it up. I gather my books and leave, gently closing the door behind me.

Just as I step from the cushy carpeting to the light hardwood in the hallway, Ella does, too. Her bedroom is across from mine: We face each other head-on. It's like looking at a life-sized picture of me in another outfit: She has the exact same tone of chestnut hair, matching dark brown eyes, the same lips that naturally frown when they're not smiling.

And they're frowning now.

Ella's eyes narrow to slits when she sees my hair. Her posture is pure pissed—underneath her plush robe, she pops a hip and rests her hand there—but more than seeing her anger, I can feel it. She exhales loudly and rolls her eyes.

"Are you done?" I ask. "We're not at auditions for a teen drama, you know. You don't have an audience."

Ella shakes her head at me.

"I mean, you're so selfish it's ridiculous," she says.

"It's just hair," I say, touching it. *Awesome hair*, I don't say. *Hair I'd like to have permanently.*

"It's not just hair," she says. "It's time. I'm up early as it is because I didn't finish everything for second half. I have to study before Betsey gets up and then teach her all of the cheers. You know there's a game next Friday! I have so much to do and now I have to flat iron my hair, too?"

"What's going on?" Betsey asks from her door, rubbing her eyes. I feel a little bad for waking her up. Her part is evening, which means that on top of being home-schooled all day, she's the one to juggle our college course, a part-time job, and cheering at night games. She goes to bed at least an hour later than we do.

When Betsey finally focuses on me, her dark eyes widen. "Seriously, Lizzie? Not again," she says with a groan.

"Not you, too," I say, eyebrows raised. She shrugs.

"Yes, her, too," Ella says. "What you do impacts all of us, Lizzie. You should remember that next time. I mean, just, thanks for this. Thanks for ruining my day." She storms downstairs, bare feet slapping gleaming wood floors all the way down.

I stifle a laugh. "Sorry," I say to Bet with a sheepish grin. "But I like it this way."

"It does look good," she says, giving me a small hug. "But I'm still going to kill you."

I stop in the entryway to gather all the stuff I need for school. I put my books in the bag. I unplug the cell phone from its charger and put it in the purse, then shove the purse in the bag, too. I shrug on the light jacket we chose for this fall and then grab the ends of the ball chain necklace and clasp it at the nape of my neck. When I straighten the weighty silver pendant so the vintage-looking pattern is facing out, there's a little twist in my torso. But as I have for the past couple of months, I ignore it.

My mom hears me turn the door handle despite the fact that she's listening to old Bon Jovi on the sound system in the kitchen. Sometimes I think she's part bat.

"Lizzie?" she calls. "Come eat some breakfast."

"I'll eat at school." I pull the door shut behind me, knowing my leaving will probably irritate her but hoping this is one of those days she lets her irritation slide. Otherwise, after school she'll probably force me into a mother/daughter heart-to-heart about the importance of proper nutrition.

Outside, it's a pretty fall day, a little hazy, but the sun's managing to peek through. I inhale the ocean air as I walk across the cobblestone driveway, looking up at the hundred-foot pines that surround the property. With the imposing trees and an iron gate, you'd think a celebrity lived here . . . until you saw our car. Apparently top on the list of "safest cars for teens," the sensible gray sedan is only just slightly better than the bus.

"Stupid old-lady car," I mutter as I climb in and buckle up.

When I turn the key, I'm simultaneously blasted by heat and music; quickly I turn down the blower and flip to the alt rock station. I can't help but laugh at Betsey's taste: She may dress like someone who lives for jam bands, but her real musical love is country. I think back to Florida, when our neighbor Nina babysat us sometimes in the afternoons so Mom could run errands without dragging along three toddlers. We'd sit out by Nina's pool listening to Reba McEntire, sipping sugary drinks we weren't allowed to have at home.

"Now, don't tell your mama, you hear?" Nina would say in her Southern accent. Practically drooling at the sight of juice boxes, we'd nod our little heads and swear on our baby dolls never to tell. Nina would sing along with Reba at the top of her lungs while Bet did backup vocals and silly dances, and I'd laugh to the point of a potty emergency.

Betsey never outgrew her affinity for country music and it's one of the things that I love about her, because it's one of the ways she's different.

Still not used to the driveway—our old house was on

a regular street—I do an Austin Powers maneuver to get the car turned in the right direction. Then I hold my breath as I drive up, hugging the right, since there's a drop-off on the left.

I wait for the gate to inch open, tossing my hair off my shoulders and finally taking a breath. For another morning, I'm safe from death by driveway. Despite my hideous sweater, I have sleek, straight hair. And now, for a few hours at least, I'm out of the house. I smile for no one to see, because these things are worth smiling about.

Two hours later, instinctively, I touch the necklace around my neck. My heart rate is up: I can hear the blood pounding in my ears. I try to calm myself as I picture the alert sounding on my mom's phone, it dragging her from whatever she's doing so she can check the GPS blip and make sure I'm where I'm supposed to be. Back in Florida when we were little, the necklace used to make me feel protected. Now, sitting here in trig, panicking because I don't know the answers, it feels invasive. Not only do I have my own stress to worry about, but I have her stress to worry about, too.

"It's a killer, isn't it?" the guy across the aisle whispers, nodding down at the quiz. He's got unfortunate acne that distracts from an otherwise solid-looking face.

"The worst," I whisper back before our teacher gives us a look and we're forced to focus. But when I do, I realize once again how little I know.

I studied; I really did. Ella is much better at math, and

6

after the requisite teasing, she helped me the past three nights. But it's too much. Going through the problems, I feel like I'm trying to read Mandarin while blindfolded. Sure, Woodbury is tougher than South was last year, but it's not like I'm an idiot. And yet, we're only a couple weeks into the school year and already, without a doubt, I can honestly say that...

I. Hate. Triangles.

And granted, I'm freaking out right now about a quiz on the first three chapters of the book, so I don't know a lot about it, but it seems to me that triangles are the very essence of trigonometry.

I spend fifty minutes suffering through the most painful academic experience of my life. Even before the bell rings, I am chastising myself for being so stupid. So flawed. Even though my mom's not my DNA donor, I was grown in her womb; her smartness should've rubbed off on me somehow.

How can I just not *get* math?

I jump at the bell, then reluctantly hand in my quiz. I jump again when my phone vibrates in my pocket; I haven't even made it to the classroom door yet. I don't check the caller ID; I know who it is.

"Hi."

"Lizzie, it's Mom," she says, trying to sound calm when I know her well enough to know that she's not.

"I know," I say, weaving around two girls blocking the door. "Hi."

Pause. "Your heart rate just shot up: What happened? You were in math class, right? Is everything okay?" The way her voice sounds right now reminds me of the time in middle school when she forgot there was a museum field trip and the tracker showed me across town during school hours.

"Geez, calm down," I say. "I'm fine. It was just a quiz."

Silence.

"Did you fail?" she asks quietly, saying "fail" like some people say "cancer." I hear her take a breath and hold it on the other end of the line and I can almost see the thoughts running through her brain. Mom places an incredibly high value on doing well in school.

"How should I know?" I say. "I only just handed it in. I won't get—"

"Lizzie, you know."

Pause.

"Yes."

She lets out her breath like a popped tire. "I'm going to come home for a few minutes after Bet's done with night class. We'll have a family meeting to discuss this."

"But, Mom, I—"

"We'll discuss it tonight," she says sharply. "I think we need to—"

Service cuts out and my bars are too low to call her back. I'm left to wonder as I leave the math corridor and head down the main hallway what Mom thinks we *need to* do this time.

After psych and government, I race to my locker, then flip around and rush toward the commons, where I'm blasted by the smell of fried foods. My stomach grumbles— it's been too long since my vending-machine breakfast— but there's no time to stop. I cut through the circular space, weaving my way around tables and kids with trays toward the exit to the student lot. I imagine Ella standing in the entryway of our house with a stopwatch, tapping her toes. The longer it takes me to get there, the less time she has.

"Hey, Elizabeth!"

I look over and see David Something from student government smiling a salesman's smile. "Take a load off," he says, his voice carrying over the lunchtime noise. The other football players at his table look at me curiously as David pats the empty seat next to him.

I smile back and wave politely but keep walking. I stifle a laugh when I hear one of David's friends say, "Burn!" just before I reach the doors.

I make it outside and check my phone for the time: I'm doing okay. Even though lots of kids go off campus for lunch, no one is nearby, so I jog to the car. I throw the bag on the passenger seat and drive home no more than five miles per hour over the posted speed limits. All I need is to get a speeding ticket the same day I fail a trig quiz.

I drive through the gates and down the driveway, then park and turn off the car but leave the keys in the ignition and the bag on the passenger seat. Ella is walking toward me before I've shut the door. With her stick-straight hair and matching cardigan and skirt, I might as well be staring at myself. Most of the time it's just how things are, but today, maybe because I'm already worried about the quiz, it's the bad kind of surreal. The only difference between us at the moment is our posture: Hers is tall and confident, mine is slumped.

"You okay?" she says when she's close enough for me to hear. "I felt it."

I nod, thinking of the sudden sense of unease that comes over me when Ella or Betsey panics about something. "Did Mom totally freak out?"

Ella glances at the front door and then refocuses on me. "A little," she admits. "I think she's just disappointed."

"Ugh," I say. "She said she's coming home for a family meeting tonight. She never comes home at night!"

When we were born, our mom gave up her real passion of being a scientist so she could work nights and be home during the day with us. Instead of doing the genetics research she loves, she's using her *other* degree to be an ER doctor, somehow functioning on three hours of sleep a night.

"I know. It's weird," Ella says, stepping forward to give me a quick hug. "But it'll be okay," she says into my hair. "We'll figure it out." Dramatic as she is, in a real crisis, Ella's always there. We pull apart and smile at each other: Mine's forced, because she's trying to lift my spirits.

10

"Anything I need to know?" she asks.

I shrug again. "Other than the trig debacle...no," I say. "Oh, wait, that guy David from student government tried to wave me over at lunch." Ella doesn't have a class with David, but she nods anyway.

"What'd he want?"

I shrug. "I don't know. I just waved back and kept going. I didn't want to make you late."

"Thanks," she says with another small smile.

"No problem. Good luck."

Ella laughs. "I've got the easy part," she says wistfully, like she misses the challenge, even though she has cheer practice, which she loves. "I think I can handle Spanish and dance."

"Don't forget creative writing," I say, the wistful one now.

"Oh, right," she says as she reaches out to unclasp the necklace from my neck. She puts it on, then hugs me goodbye and goes to the car. I walk across the cobblestones and, from the front porch, turn back to watch Ella go. It's like I'm having an out-of-body experience—like I'm watching myself. Except that Ella drives straight up the middle of the driveway, fearless.

And I love her for it.

The rest of the day is like clockwork. I spend three hours at homeschool with Betsey and my all-business mother (who through pursed lips refuses to acknowledge what happened in trig whatsoever during "school time").

We trudge through the same subjects that Ella's studying at Woodbury, just like Ella and Betsey did with my morning schedule. When Mom leaves for work at 3:30, I crank the music in our home gym for the same treadmill session that Bet and Ella did earlier, while Bet catches up on chemistry. Ella returns after cheer practice, and shortly after that, Bet leaves for night class. Ella and I eat dinner and do homework, comparing notes and chatting casually until Bet comes home again.

Then I get nervous.

"She'll be here anytime now," I whisper, seconds before the door opens downstairs.

"You're totally psychic," Betsey says with a laugh, but I'm not in the mood. Instead, I try to judge my mother's level of pissed-ness by the way she kicks off her shoes and rushes up the stairs.

"Oh, good, you're all here," she says when she rounds the corner to the rec room. Her hair is pulled back at her neck and she's wearing ill-fitting but remarkably clean scrubs with a cardigan over them.

"Hi, Mom," I say as she hurries into the room and sits down on the couch next to Ella. She pats Ella's knee, smiles at Betsey, then frowns when her eyes meet mine.

"Hi, Lizzie," she says before sighing like I'm the absolute worst there is for not knowing about stupid freaking triangles. "I don't have a lot of time, so let's get right to it."

"You should have just told us whatever you wanted to

say when you saw us earlier," Ella says. "Don't you have patients?"

"I wanted to talk to all three of you at once," Mom says, making me feel sick. That doesn't sound good at all. "And besides, earlier I was still figuring out what to do." She pauses for breath, glancing at the clock on the wall.

"What do you mean, 'figuring out what to do'?" Ella asks, looking suddenly concerned.

Mom faces her. "I've decided we're going to make a change in light of Lizzie's... challenge," she says. I can feel Ella glance at me, but I keep my eyes on Mom. No one else speaks, so she continues.

"First, I want to say that we're lucky that it's taken this long for noticeable differences to crop up," she says. "I was fearful every day through puberty, and yet thankfully, that wasn't an issue." I don't have to look at the others to know they're blushing, too. Nobody wants to hear their mother say the word *puberty*.

Mom goes on.

"But now, it's grown obvious to me that Lizzie is developing more right-brain tendencies," she says, looking into my eyes. "I'm sorry, Lizzie, I thought that by allowing you to be the one in those classes at school, you'd grasp them more easily. I thought maybe I was doing a poor job of teaching them. But it seems that math and science just aren't your forte." Mom gives me a sympathetic smile that's completely annoying.

"But if today is any indication, our current setup isn't working," she continues. "We're not even three weeks in and already it's clear that to remain on this path could draw attention to us, and therefore threaten everything. Because of this," Mom says, shifting like she's bracing for a triple teen outburst, "I am switching junior year assignments."

I feel myself stiffen; Ella sucks in her breath.

"Are you serious?" Betsey asks. Mom nods.

"Ella will take first half," she says authoritatively, but not meeting Ella's eyes, probably because she knows how disappointed Ella's going to be to miss out on cheer practice. "Lizzie will take second half. Betsey, you'll stay with evenings." Betsey visibly relaxes in her chair.

"But we have the schedule down," Ella says in protest. "This isn't fair."

"I know," Mom says. "But you've made straight A's your whole life. You just transferred—and Principal Cowell specifically commented on your high marks. If suddenly you start getting C's in math, it'll attract attention. And beyond that, it's time to start thinking of college. Of your future."

Start thinking of college? I feel like she's been thinking of college since we were two days old. The funny thing is that none of us knows how we'll even handle college logistically, so we've all just put our heads in the sand about it. I blow out my breath, but everyone ignores me.

"So, it's settled then," Mom says, checking the clock again as she stands up. "I've got to get back to the hospital."

"How soon?" I ask, knowing that I need to brush up on the cheers Ella's learned so far. My stomach lurches at the thought of manufacturing pep.

"I called the school and told them that you had a migraine today," Mom says. "I talked them into letting you retake the quiz."

Nerves rage in my insides—I can feel mine, and the others', too. She can't be saying what I think she's saying. "How soon, Mom?" I ask again.

She looks at the clock one more time, then looks back at me.

"Tomorrow."

two

"Don't forget to take off your nail polish."

Mom's talking to me from the kitchen doorway on the morning of the most last-minute, massive switch we've ever done. It's ironic that she's nagging me: She's the one who left five minutes ago to mail bills before homeschool, then came back because she forgot both the bills and her car keys. I roll my eyes at her and she leaves, then I look down at my perfectly painted white nails.

"Why do yours always chip so easily?" I ask Ella, frowning. She shrugs, her eyes on the valley below our house. I know she's upset about the switch, too. She stands and takes her cereal bowl to the sink before disappearing, probably to brush her teeth. Again. I shove back and go upstairs, then wander down the hall toward Mom's room in search of remover.

I open the door to the cool, dark room and flip on the overhead light. As I squish across the carpet, I glance over at the three baby portraits in thick brown wooden frames, hung art-gallery straight on the wall with the door. I feel a familiar prickling on the back of my neck as I stop for a long look.

Anyone else would see the same kid wearing different outfits and expressions, but really, it's different people. Ella's openmouthed; Mom said she was mesmerized by a butterfly on a stick that the photographer used to get her attention. Her background is department store all the way. In her photo, Betsey's drooling like a Saint Bernard. And I'm crying, probably because someone put me in a bucket.

What makes the hairs on my neck and arms stand up is that there's another picture in a drawer somewhere— just a four-by-six snapshot taken by a proud parent—and the baby in the photo looks identical to the babies on the wall. Somewhere, there's a photo of the Original, the baby who died.

The baby Mom cloned to make us.

"What are you doing in here?" Bet asks behind me, scaring me so badly that I bang my shoulder on the wall when I jump back. "Sorry," she says, laughing. Bet's always been a fan of frightening others.

"I'm getting nail polish remover," I say, turning away from the faces that started as someone else's.

"And visiting the Wall of Fame," Bet says, waving at the photos. "God, Ella was a weird-looking baby."

I chuckle, then we're quiet a second. "Doesn't it ever freak you out?"

"What?" Bet asks.

"That we're not...normal," I say.

"Lizzie, don't be dumb. We're normal," Betsey says, shaking her head at me. "We just happened to be cloned instead of made the regular way."

"I don't know," I say. "Sometimes it makes me feel inferior."

"Well, it shouldn't," Bet says. "You're awesome. But you know what? Mom's going to make us both feel inferior if we don't get our homework done because we're standing around gawking at our baby selves. You're already on her list this week; why make it worse? Let's go."

I allow myself to be dragged by the hand toward the door of Mom's room, wondering whether the kids at school would consider clones unnatural; wondering what they'd think if they knew the truth. My fingernails are still painted, and as I flip off the light behind me, my neck is still prickling, too.

"Here," Ella says, holding out the necklace at lunch. We're on the front porch and the car is idling; I was the one waiting this time.

"Thanks," I say, taking it and putting it on, thinking that to anyone else, the necklace probably looks like a family heirloom: a locket containing tiny photos of those I love. But it's a lot more than that.

"Everything go okay this morning?" I ask.

"Yeah, fine," Ella says, blowing out her breath. "Classes were okay; I talked to that David guy a little in student government." She pauses, eyeing me for a few seconds before adding, "And...I aced the quiz."

Ella wrote down the classroom numbers, but still, I'm edgy as I walk into Spanish III that afternoon. Instinctively, I make my way to our seat: front row, closest to the right wall. It's the one we choose in any classroom, assuming we're given a choice. We do it mostly for convenience's sake—sometimes someone gets sick and we need to fill in for each other—but I'm not saying one of us (ahem, Betsey) doesn't have a few obsessive-compulsive tendencies, too.

I settle into the chair, lean back, and twirl an end of my hair, pretending to be bored. As far as everyone else knows, this is my sixth class of the day, not my first. I try to look tired, even faking a yawn just before Mr. Sanchez shows up. He drops his teachers' manual loudly on the front podium, then addresses the class.

"*Hola, estudiantes!*" he shouts, beaming like we're his favorite people on earth. He claps his hands loudly a few times, probably trying to shock us, with our post-lunch comas, into the afternoon. Happy to be learning Spanish from a native speaker instead of my mom, I'm okay with his antics.

"*Hola,* Señor Sanchez," I reply aloud. No one else

responds. A few people snicker. Mr. Sanchez looks at me with eyebrows raised, smiling.

"Brownnoser," a girl mutters behind me.

I don't turn to see who said it, but I learn my lesson. For the rest of the class period, I only respond when called upon. But that doesn't mean I don't shout out the answers in my head. And, unlike in trigonometry, here I get them all right.

One step removed from private, Woodbury is one of the few remaining public schools with an arts program, still offering things like music, painting, pottery, and dance. I may not want to chant "Go, TEAM!" while wearing a revealing outfit, but I've always loved every form of dance. So, inheriting our dance elective from Ella was a gift.

Seventh period, I walk confidently to the studio in the hallway next to the gym without pausing to think or ask for directions. It's possible that I might have happened to take the very long way to history once or twice to see what the dancers were up to. Thankfully, now it's my turn.

I find locker number 27—it was assigned—and type in the only combination we ever use: 3, 33, 13. Inside, I find a black halter dance top with a built-in bra, black drawstring shorts that, embarrassingly, say DANCE across the butt, a red hoodie shrug that covers my arms and upper back, footless nude tights, and black, broken-in jazz shoes. Faster than fast, I change, excited to get to try out the dances Ella's already taught me with a room full of other students.

"I hope she finally teaches us the ending today," a redhead named Alison says from behind me as I walk from the locker room to the dance area. I've seen her before during first half: She always says hello when we pass in the halls.

"I know," I say, thankful for Ella's prep, "we've been stuck on the middle section for a week!"

"I think it's easier to dance the whole thing," Alison says. "I'd rather learn all of it and practice it straight through than keep stopping to perfect each section."

"Totally," I say, feeling a little awkward but forcing myself to remember that even though I don't know Alison, she thinks she knows me. "And you know how if you learn something then sleep on it, you'll remember it better?" She nods. "Well, I bet if she teaches us the ending today, we'll all nail the dance tomorrow."

"Genius," Alison says, smiling warmly.

"Hardly," I say, laughing as I pull my long hair into a knot at the back of my head, checking for strays in the wall of mirrors.

"Showtime," Alison says as the teacher takes her place.

And for forty-five minutes, I'm in heaven.

I leave my hair pulled back for creative writing, because it's sweaty and I used all my shower time going over the routine—the whole routine—three more times with Alison. Still high on dance, Madonna ringing in my ears, I walk into the creative writing classroom and cut straight to the front desk on the right. Not until I'm practically in the lap of the desk's occupant do I realize that it's taken. I stop short, no clue what to do. *Should I just sit in a free seat or run out of the room and call Ella?* While I'm deciding, the guy in my seat feels my stare and turns around.

Suddenly I notice that the room has grown very warm.

"Hi?" he asks, smiling with his brow furrowed. I don't know him, but his greeting seems to be translatable to *Gawk much?*

He moves in a funny way, almost levitating the desk while he's still in it. Then he makes the walls ripple, too. *How does he do that?* I wonder, but not for long, because the floor buckles. I reach out for the desk next to me; we're having an earthquake. Except no one else seems to be alarmed.

"Are you okay?" I hear the guy ask.

I don't answer.

Instead, I pass out.

When I wake up seconds or minutes later, my classmates are looking at me from their desks, some of them smirking, some of them concerned. My first thought is that I'm thankful that I'm not wearing a skirt. My second thought is of the necklace. My hand flies to my throat, and for once this week, I catch a break: The necklace isn't there. I must have left it in my gym locker after dance.

"Elizabeth?" Mr. Ames says, standing over me, concerned. "Are you all right?"

"I'm fine," I mutter, feeling like an idiot. I look at Guy, who's half out of his seat; he eases back down.

"Are you sure?" Mr. Ames asks. "You look quite pale."

It's weird to be on the floor while he's hovering over

me like this; I can see up his prominent nose. I start to sit up and choose to look back at Guy while I do it.

That's when I realize that he's actually pretty cute. Except not in the traditional way. Picking apart the pieces, he's too angular. His chin and mouth are sharp; his nose looks like it started out perfectly straight then met up with a tree or another guy's shoulder at some point. His hair can only be described as a side spike, like he stood sideways in front of a fan blowing hairspray instead of air. He's tall and towering even seated, watching me curiously with light brown eyes. Just as I decide that he looks like the daytime alter ego for a nighttime superhero, he speaks.

"She hit the ground pretty hard," he says in a low, smooth voice. "Maybe she needs to go to see Miss Brady."

"Excellent idea," Mr. Ames says, nodding. "Let me help you up, Elizabeth," he says, offering me a hand. Then, to everyone else, "Who wants to volunteer to walk her to the nurse's office?"

"No!" I say, jumping up. I can't go to the nurse's office. She'll call my mom, who will make me go home and then prescribe chicken broth and a bedtime earlier than a toddler's. "Really, I'm fine," I say. "I had dance last period and overdid it. I just got a little light-headed." Mr. Ames is frowning at me, so I add, "I didn't eat lunch."

"Well, at least go get a snack," he says, shaking his head. "You girls." I can't help but wonder whether he thinks I'm anorexic or something.

"Great," I say quickly. "I'll go right now."

"Someone needs to go with you," he says, "just to make sure you're all right. Anyone?" He and I both look around the class; no one volunteers. I don't blame them: We're only a few weeks into the school year and I didn't go here last year. Technically, I'm still new.

"I'll do it," Guy volunteers. The hairs on my arms stand up.

"That would be fantastic," Mr. Ames says. Even in my slightly woozy state, I wonder: *Really? Fantastic?*

Mr. Ames writes us hall passes and hands them over. "Take your time."

My legs are shaky as I turn to leave the room; Guy follows me. Mr. Ames resumes class before we're to the doorway. "As for everyone else, please open your notebooks for a fun new writing assignment. I'd like you to write two pages that begin with the phrase, 'It all started when the dog . . .'"

Guy laughs under his breath. Once we're out in the hallway, I turn and face him.

"Thanks for coming with me," I say. "But really, I'm fine. You can just hang out if you want."

"No worries," he says with that easy voice that seems to float over to my ears. "I'm hungry, too."

"Oh, okay." Now I get it: I'm nothing but a free pass to the vending machines. Even so, although we just met, I fight to keep from smiling in his presence.

We walk down the long spoke of the English hallway in silence. I desperately want to ask his name, but I can't be sure that Ella hasn't already, so I keep my mouth shut. Though we don't speak, I am aware of everything: the hint of a strut in his step; the way he genuinely greets the few people that pass like he knows everyone in school; the way he laughs after pulling out his iPhone and scrolling around for a second.

"There's a ghost in this hallway," he says, tilting the screen so I can see the "ghost meter" app.

"I hope you didn't pay for that."

"Naw, it's free, but I've paid for worse," he says before moving to hold open the door to the center of the school for me. Woodbury is a sprawling wheel with all of the departments branching out from the common/cafeteria area.

"Thanks." He nods with a half smile. When we reach the vending machines, he puts away his iPhone and pulls a few dollars from his pocket.

"What's your poison?" he asks, gesturing toward the rows of candy, chips, granola bars, and beverages.

"You don't have to buy my food." This makes him smile full-out, which zaps me like I'm sticking a butter knife in a light socket, but in a good way.

"You left your bag in class."

I look down, as if it would be dangling from my neck if I had it with me. But he's right; I have no money. "Fine, then I'll take a Twix."

"Good choice." He buys two Twix bars and two bottles of water and hands me my half.

"Thank you."

"Least I can do," he says.

"Huh?" I unwrap my candy while he does. "What do you mean?"

"I missed," he says. When I scrunch up my face at him, he clarifies. "I tried to catch you, but I missed. The least I can do is buy you a candy bar."

"How chivalrous of you." I can't help but laugh.

"Can I record you saying that and play it back for my mom?" We start back toward class.

"Sure," I say, wanting to add something witty but coming up dry.

We're quiet again through the English hallway, but just before the door to our classroom, he turns to face me.

"You look different today."

"Uh..." I'm not sure what to say. I'm frozen, gripping my water bottle, probably with chocolate in my teeth.

"Not in a bad way," he says. "Good different."

"Oh."

He pauses for a second, like he might say more, but then he nods toward the door and walks into the classroom. I follow behind, the plastic bottle protesting in my viselike grip. Once again, I'm relieved that I'm not wearing the necklace: I'm pretty sure my heart rate just surged to somewhere near the red zone. As I sit down in the only open desk in the classroom—the one right behind Guy—I think about the enormity of what just happened.

Maybe for the first time in my life, someone noticed.

He noticed me.

three

"Hey, you know that guy in creative writing?" I ask Ella the next morning at breakfast. "The one with the hair? He sits in our usual seat? Thanks for the warning about that, by the way."

She looks at me funny, maybe because she's clueless, probably because she's wondering why I'm asking. On the verge of blushing, I start buttering my toast so I have something else to focus on.

"Yeah?" she asks. "What about him?"

"He said hi to me and I felt like a moron because I didn't know his name."

Ella just stares at me.

I roll my eyes at her. "Ella!" I shout. "Quit messing around. What's his name?"

She laughs a little, stands, and takes her plate to the sink. I think she's going to ignore me completely, but halfway through the doorway, she says his name over her shoulder.

"Sean Kelly."

I use the last ten minutes of dance class primping instead of rehearsing. After my speed shower, I pull my hair back into a wet knot and then hurry to creative writing, charged by the thought of seeing a guy I don't know at all. He doesn't arrive until just before the bell, but when Mr. Ames turns to write today's vocabulary words on the board, he turns around in his desk.

My desk.

"Hey, Elizabeth." *Zap.*

"Hi, Sean," I say back, swallowing butterflies. I want to say his whole name, but that would be elementary school–style immature, so I just think it.

Hi, Sean Kelly.

I solo brainstormed a few conversation starters on the way to school, but unfortunately class starts, so I don't get the chance to try them out. Sean's forced to turn around and I'm obligated to stare at his broad back for most of class, pausing only to make periodic eye contact with Mr. Ames so he doesn't call me out. I manage to stay under the radar. But then at the bell, Mr. Ames *does* call me out: He asks me to hang back after class for a few minutes. Disappointed, I glance at Sean as he leaves the room, then walk up front.

"Thanks for sticking around, Elizabeth," Mr. Ames says. "I won't make you late for your next class—I just wanted to tell you how fantastic I thought your dog story was."

"Really?" I ask, ignoring his overuse of *fantastic*.

"Definitely," he says with a warm smile as he starts straightening papers on his podium. "It was an improvement over last week's assignment and..."

Stomach flip. *I'm better than Ella at something.*

"...I just wanted to say that I'm expecting big things from you this year."

"Wow," I say sheepishly. "That's really...thanks, Mr. Ames." No teacher has ever pulled me aside to tell me that I'm doing a good job before. Strangely, it makes me want to head home and start tonight's homework right this second.

"No problem," Mr. Ames says. "See you tomorrow."

"See you tomorrow," I echo as I turn and leave the classroom. I'm so deep in my happy place that I nearly collide with someone when I step into the hall. It takes a second before I realize that someone is Sean.

"Are you in trouble?"

Were you waiting for me? I wonder.

"No," I say. "He told me he liked my dog story."

"Did he say it was *fantastic*?" Sean asks, which makes me burst out laughing.

"Actually, he did!"

"That's awesome," Sean says, shoving off the wall. He stuffs his iPhone into his pocket, then hoists his bag onto his shoulder. He starts walking beside me, confirming that he was, in fact, waiting. "Where are you off to now?"

"Cheerleading," I say, trying to keep the negative tone out of my voice. I mean, the squad members are fine—nice, even. The captain, Grayson Jennings, is firm but fair. It's just that I'm not into the idea of being catapulted into the air with nothing but a few skinny girls to catch me on the way down.

Sean nods in a way that annoys me, like he thinks I belong at cheerleading.

"What do you do after school?" I ask, a little snippily. He laughs.

"Whatever," he says. "Hang out with friends. Read. Play games. Write. Sometimes I take pictures."

"Of what?" I ask, tone gone.

"Well, I take all the pictures for the school Facebook," he says. "But I really like to shoot stuff around town. My mom's a pro photographer for like businesses and magazines and stuff, and sometimes she lets me help out."

"Sounds fun," I say, trying to come off as nonchalant when I really want to launch into game-show-host mode and ask him a lightning round of personal questions. But, as if we were beamed here, too soon we're at the entrance to the locker room.

"This is where I leave you," he says, nodding to the GIRLS sign over the door.

"Thanks...uh...for walking me here," I say, feeling self-conscious about the way I'm standing, the sound of my voice. Everything.

"Sure," he says. "Catch you later."

And then he turns and walks away, not too slowly or too quickly. He just goes, comfortable being him, backpack slung over his shoulder like a normal kid with a normal life.

Just...normal.

Betsey has major cramps tonight, so Ella and I draw straws for evening. It's Wednesday, so that means Freshman English 1A at the community college, but both of us would practically sit through anything for a chance to see stars. It's not like we're banned from going out at night or anything, it's just that only one of us can be out at a time.

Of course, Ella wins. Smirking, she pulls back her hair, because mine is still tangled from dance, puts on the locket, and bounces out the front door like Tigger.

I love her, but she's a total pain sometimes.

The only good thing about losing the draw is that I get to spend some alone time with Betsey. We used to spend our afternoons together but now we're ships in the night. Yesterday, we only saw each other during the few morning homeschool classes before I had to take off for second half. When I returned, she immediately left for evening. In a way, I'm glad she isn't feeling well tonight.

"So, what's going on?" I ask her when I join her in the rec room. She's squinting at the TV, because even though the front of our house is shrouded in pine trees, the back overlooks the valley below and the setting sun is casting such a harsh glare on the screen that you can hardly make out the images.

"Just suffering," Betsey says. She has a heating pad on her midsection and a bowl of ice cream in her hands. My period started this morning, too, like I'm sure Ella's did. The difference is that to us, it's nothing.

"I'm sorry, Bet," I sympathize. "Do you want anything?"

"I want the stupid sun to go away," she says. "Can you make that happen?"

I stand up and pull closed the heaviest drapes in the world: the kind you see in hotel rooms that start at the tip-top of the room and refuse to let in the tiniest smidgen of light. We stayed in two hotels on the drive from Florida to California and loved the room service and indoor swimming pools.

"Done," I say as I flop back onto the couch opposite Betsey's. "What are we watching?"

"You pick," she says, tossing me the remote. "I don't have the energy to flip."

I start changing channels but don't find anything, so I end up back where we started. When the half hour turns, a rerun of Friends begins. It's extremely funny to the point that my side hurts I'm laughing so hard. At the first commercial break, I begin the chatter again.

"So, are there any cute guys at night class?" I ask. Betsey shrugs from her sickbed.

"Not really," she says. "They're all nerds trying to get ahead."

"Like us."

"I guess," Betsey says. "Sometimes I wonder if it's worth it...there might be better things to do with our Monday and Wednesday nights."

"Like what?"

"I don't know," she says. "Skydiving. Miniature golfing. Things that are fun."

"You want to go skydiving at night?" I ask, laughing.

"You know what I mean."

"Yeah," I say, nodding. "I wonder what Mom would say if we asked to go skydiving."

Betsey looks at me and we both burst into laughter at the ridiculousness of the idea. When we've recovered, she says quietly, "I think Mom overreacted about the whole quiz thing." I look back at the TV; the commercials are on mute. "Switching our schedules and all."

"Me, too," I say, not really wanting to talk about Mom. Thankfully, the show comes back on. But then it's hard for me to pay attention; I'm distracted by memories.

"How about in second half?" Bet interrupts my thoughts. I focus and realize that we're already at another

33

commercial break. I look at her quizzically. "Guys?" she explains. And then thoughts of Mom are gone, replaced by Sean. My face must give it away, because she sets down her ice-cream bowl and sits up excitedly.

"Tell me!" she says. I'm grinning so hard I have to take a deep breath to relax my face so the words can come out.

"His name is Sean and I sit behind him in creative writing," I report. Bet's eyes are wide and sparkling like a little girl's. "He's adorable, but in an unexpected way. And tall, but he doesn't hunch over or anything. And he's super nice and funny and he waited for me after class to walk me to cheer."

"Ohmygod, what else?"

"Let's see...he's a little obsessed with his iPhone, but he's into creative stuff like obviously writing but photography, too, and did I mention he looks like a superhero?"

"Like Superman?"

"More like a less nerdy Clark Kent," I say. "No, wait, he's like Clark Kent's less nerdy son who fronts an indie rock band."

"Is he in a band?" Betsey asks, her voice high-pitched.

"No, I don't think so," I say. "But he's super cool."

"And you like him," Betsey says in a dreamlike voice, as if she's caught up in a particularly great movie love scene instead of talking about my life.

"I do," I agree, admitting it to myself and to Betsey at the same time.

"Wow."

We sit, staring at nothing for a moment, both of us probably wondering what it would be like to actually date someone. Betsey's the one who mentions it.

"We should ask again," she says. "I think it's time. Elizabeth Best is the only girl in school who doesn't date. It's weird."

"She'll say no," I say, remembering the last time. At South, a guy named Shane Williams asked Betsey to Homecoming after their social studies class one day (Betsey did second half last year). Mom said no before the question was even out of Bet's mouth.

"Yeah, but we were only fifteen then, and you know how overprotective she is," Bet says. "Plus she was freaked out because she thought our next-door neighbor was spying on us. I get it. I mean, she could go to jail if anyone knew about us. But it's different now. We're more careful. We're seventeen."

"Not until January," I say, giving her a funny look, then refocusing on the TV. "And I don't know, Bet. I don't think she'll go for it."

"I'm doing it," Betsey says. "I'm bringing it up."

After not even ibuprofen works, Betsey goes to bed early. I turn off the TV and lazily drag myself to my room with the cozy throw blanket still wrapped around my shoulders. I decide to check our Facebook—the Facebook that

35

we had to beg Mom to let us have, the Facebook that she only consented to because one of our teachers at South posted extra-credit assignments there sometimes.

Of course, it's only *one* account.

I log on and check the notifications, knowing well that I can't reply to any of the comments since Ella's the one "on" tonight, but at least I can troll the pages and kill some time before bed. I make sure that I'm hidden from view in case people know that Elizabeth Best takes a college course right now, then I scan the updates. Ella posted to the page five minutes before class.

Elizabeth Best is admiring the amazing moon on the way to night class.

Just as I'm silently cursing Ella for rubbing it in, a little alert in the upper left corner catches my eye: We have a friend request. It could be anyone, so I'm unsuspecting when I click on the link and see who it's from.

Sean Kelly.

I suck in my breath and hold it as I click to accept the request, then I go to his page and look around. He has 530 friends; I try not to feel inadequate. His status updates are frequent and funny, and I'm not surprised to find quite a few photo albums.

I click through his pictures and notice two things: He's photogenic, and a lot of his pictures feature him and other girls. A pit forms in my stomach at the sight of Sean dressed for a dance with Grayson Jennings next to him. He's so magnetic; of course he dated the sweet, beautiful, all-around-perfect captain of the cheerleading squad.

Just, of course.

Another of his photo albums shows off his photography. There are expertly framed landscapes, funky old trains, elderly people in rockers, and shots of kids at a carnival taken from odd angles with vintage filters. Halfway through the album, I click Next and find a *Seventeen* magazine–worthy close-up of Grayson. She is freckle-faced and smiling in the sunshine with a flower in her hair. It almost makes me want to die until I remember that at practice yesterday, she talked about how she's dating Cooper someone. But still, how can a third of a person compete with one whole Grayson?

A little flag appears in the corner of my screen, telling me that I have a new personal message. Adrenaline shoots through me when I see that it's from Sean.

Sean Kelly   About 1 minute ago
Hi Elizabeth,
Wow, your name is long. You are in mad need of a nickname.
What's going on? I see that you're at night class.
What are you taking? Write back if you can.

My heart is thump, thump, thumping under my ribcage and it won't stop. I stare at the empty box awaiting my reply, unsure what to do. *I can't reply...or can I? He might think that it's just me, Elizabeth, replying from class. But what if Ella logs on and posts something contradictory? No, she won't. She's too studious.*

Undecided, I shove back from the computer and leave the room. I go downstairs, mostly to buy myself some thinking time. Directionless, I head to the kitchen and open the fridge. I grab a soda and then hit the cupboard for some chips, which I start nervously crunching by the handful.

Back in my room, I sit down and reread his note. I wipe my salty chip hands on my pants, then, impulsively, I type.

Elizabeth Best   5 minutes ago
Hi Sean,
Thanks for friending me. As for my name, personally, I don't have a problem with Elizabeth, but if you are spelling or typing challenged, feel free to nickname me. But it had better be good.
Yes, I'm at class. I'm taking Freshman English 1A this semester and 1B next semester. Probably Freshman Math next year so I'll have two classes done by the time I start college. My mom is really, really concerned about me getting into a good college. ☺

I sit and stare at the message. It's already longer than his original note, which makes me want to edit myself.

But instead of overthinking things, I just hit Reply. Minutes later, another message from him comes in.

Sean Kelly   2 minutes ago
I won't keep bugging you. I don't want to get you
kicked out of class. But I'll think of a wicked
nickname for sure. See you in writing tomorrow.

It's nice . . . but disappointing. I want to write back that he's not bugging me, that I want to talk all night. But he thinks I'm in class, and besides, that would sound desperate. Instead, I just write back "See you tomorrow" and leave it at that.

I get up and brush my teeth, thinking that the exchange left me happy and sad at the same time, like a ball of protons and electrons, and I can't believe I just thought of that analogy, maybe I'm not so stupid after all, Mom.

When I go back to turn off the computer, I notice that Ella's done with class and has updated her status again. I happen to be looking at her comment when another one comes in.

Sean Kelly How about Astro Girl, you know, cause you
like the moon? No, that's just as long as Elizabeth. I'll
keep thinking.

I stifle a giggle at the thought of Sean trying to come up with nicknames for me, then I realize something and get nervous. From his comment, Ella will surely know that I was online when I wasn't supposed to be. Just as I'm considering calling her from the landline, another comment comes through.

This one's from ... David?

David Chancellor Hey you. Don't forget what we talked about. See you in govt.

WHAT? What is "Don't forget what we talked about"? What does that mean? I decide to wait until Ella gets home to ask her about it, and I don't have to wait long: She shows up a lot quicker than it usually takes Betsey to return from class. Suddenly Ella's looming in my bedroom doorway, and she's annoyed.

"What's up with being online while it was my time?" she asks, hands on hips.

"What's up with David?"

"What's up with *Sean*?"

We simultaneously blush in exactly the same way— blotches spreading over our foreheads and the apples of our cheeks—effectively sharing the details of our secret crushes without having to utter the words. Ella hesitates a moment before coming over and flopping down on my bed. She grabs my hand and we lie next to each other on our backs, hands clasped between us. A few minutes pass before she speaks.

"It's pointless," she says quietly. Defeated.

"It is," I agree, a feeling of angst sitting hard on me. It's an unfamiliar one, though, like wanting something back that I never had in the first place.

"Unless..." Ella says, even quieter still. My head snaps to look at her; she stares at the ceiling.

"Unless what?" I ask.

"Nothing," she says quickly, then, "Just what if we could go back to pretending to be triplets like when we were little? What if we could live normally again?"

Ella's words give form to what's been eating me for the past few months: the thing that I haven't let myself acknowledge. The fact that maybe after all this time, I'm starting to think it's wrong for us to live as one person. The fact that I've been wondering about—almost craving—change. But knowing all that Mom's given up for us—her career, any sort of a social life—it feels blasphemous.

"That's too risky," I say. "What if they found us?"

"They can't possibly still be looking for us," Ella says. "It's been seven years since the trial."

"We both know Mom's paranoid," I say with a sigh, "but she's pretty positive they still are."

Ella's quiet for a while, and when I hear someone speak, I'm surprised that it's me. "What should we do about it?" I ask. It's Ella's turn to look at me, excitement on her face.

"Should we talk to her?"

I shake my head. "I'm not sure it'll help."

"Then what?"

41

"I don't know," I say. "But something. We have to do something . . . right?"

We're quiet again for a little while, both staring at the ceiling and lost in separate but probably similar thoughts. Ella and I breathe at matching meter; we sound exactly the same. It's easy to get hypnotized by synchronicity, and soon enough, I'm nodding off.

"Can I sleep in here tonight?" Ella asks, bringing me back to awake.

"Of course," I say sleepily, because I want to be there for her. And I don't want to be alone, either.

four

"All right, everyone, today we're going to critique one another's dog stories," Mr. Ames says at the beginning of creative writing. I'm trying hard to listen, but Sean's back is distracting; somehow I force myself to focus on our teacher. "The goal this semester is to keep working on the stories and see how far we get with them." I smile at the thought of going into the holiday break with a solid start to a book.

Mr. Ames tells us to pick partners.

Turn around, Sean. Ask to be my partner.

"Want to work together?" he asks seconds after I think it. I smile and nod, and out of the corner of my eye, I see letdown on several faces across the aisle. I guess Sean's equally charming to girls and guys alike.

After the slightest hint of hesitation on my part—no one's read my writing except teachers and family—we trade papers and read quietly. I smile through his two pages, which are cleverly written from the perspective of a furious cat who asserts that the arrival of the dog has ruined her life.

"This is really funny," I say when I'm finished. I look up at Sean and he's staring at me intently. "I think it's awesome."

"You stole my line," he says. "Yours is great, too. It's better than mine."

"It is *not*," I say, rolling my eyes at him. "Anyway, it's based on a true story of a toad-sucking dog. It was on the news. The toads gave off this juice from their skin that was like a drug to the dog. He was addicted!"

"That's the weirdest thing I've ever heard," Sean says. "I thought you made it up."

"No," I say, a little embarrassed. "It would've been better if I did."

"Naw," Sean says. "Everyone finds inspiration in real life. You put your own spin on the story; it was really great."

"Thanks, Sean," I say.

"You're welcome, Beth."

Without meaning to, I flinch. Hard.

I have no idea what the Original's name was—Mom says she never knew—but I've always thought of her as

Beth. Beth is the name of a little girl trapped in time; it's perfectly tragic, like Beth March in Little Women.

Sean holds up his hands.

"Whoa," he says quietly. "I get it. No Beth."

I shake my head, feeling stupid. He must think I'm one of those melodramatic girls. I take a deep breath and smile warmly. "Sorry."

"No worries," he says. "So, Queenie..."

I frown. "Seriously?"

"Fine...just Elizabeth," he says.

"Good. And yes?"

"Do you want go to lunch tomorrow?"

The good kind of shiver shoots up my spine and down my arms. I want nothing more than to spend some time alone with Sean, getting to know him better. And yet, how can I possibly eat lunch with him? By the time I make it to school, the lunch period is more than halfway over. He'll probably want to meet me at my locker after fifth period, but that's just not possible...unless Ella does it.

No way.

Sean is looking at me, waiting for my response. I'm taking too long, but put on the spot like this, I just can't figure out how to make it work.

"I'm really sorry," I say finally, long after the moment has passed. "I'd love to, but I have plans tomorrow."

"Oh," Sean says, nodding at me like it's no big deal. But I see a flicker of disappointment in his eyes.

"Twenty minutes," Mr. Ames calls to the class.

"Guess we'd better get back to it," Sean says.

"Guess so."

And with that, we both look back to the papers in front of us and reread, pens in hand to make notes. Or at least, I try to. I can't help wanting to rewind ten minutes and do it better. I could have figured something out. But now it seems like I may have lost my chance.

Later, frustrated by the feeling that there's no way I can have a future with Sean, all I can think of is the past. How my family and I got to this point. When I stare up at my night-black ceiling, I remember when Mom came to wake me.

"Lizzie," she whispered. "Lizzie, honey, wake up."

"What?" I asked, foggy from having been asleep for only a couple of hours. I'd read long past bedtime.

"I'm going to get you a suitcase. You need to put your special clothes and toys into it and get ready to go. We're leaving."

"Where are we going?" I asked, yawning.

"To California," Mom said.

"Why?" I asked. I remember not really feeling alarmed, just curious.

"There are people looking for us," Mom said. "We have to leave this house and this town so they don't find us. And we need to start playing a game—we're going to start pretending that you and your sisters are just one person. Doesn't that sound fun?"

"Okay," I said, not really thinking it sounded fun. But I was a good girl, one who basically accepted things and went with what Mom said. I packed, as did the others, and we left in the middle of the night without ninety percent of our belongings. I'm still not sure what happened to most of it.

Until then, I'd thought I was a triplet.

Little by little, it all came out after that.

And now, little by little, I'm starting to wish I could send it back to wherever it came from.

five

The next day, when I pull into the student lot halfway through lunchtime, I have to circle around three times to find a spot. Ella's crush David—*Dave*, as she calls him—is parking three spaces down. He gets out of a silver Lexus, which I hope is one of his parents', and jogs over, carrying a bulging fast food bag that looks like it might explode.

"Hungry?" I say, nodding to the sack. He laughs loudly.

"Ha ha," he says, in case I didn't hear him actually laughing. "It's not all for me. It was my turn to pick up lunch for the debate team."

Of course he's on the debate team.

"Cool," I say, pretending for Ella's sake that I care.

I look at David in the reflection on the outside of the building as we approach, wondering what on earth Ella sees in him. I mean, okay, he's nice-looking enough in a straitlaced sort of way. His hair is blondish brown and combed. His eyes are a standard-issue blue that some people might find welcoming. His shoulders are broad. He's athletic. But somehow, I just don't see him the way Ella does. David is that guy who'll play professional football and then own his own car dealership, or become mayor or something. He's not me. My preference is more...

"Sean!" I shout when he bursts through the doors, three guys trailing behind him. He smiles, and I try not to blush my face off for shouting his name like a groupie.

"What's up, Elizabeth?" His tone is casual, but I can tell that he's happy to see me, too. He stops walking and one of his friends almost runs into him.

"Dude," the friend says.

"You're the one tailgating," Sean says to him, laughing, but his eyes stay on me. But then Sean notices David. And his supersized lunch sack. And my very Lizzie-style ensemble that Ella and Betsey let me choose last night. And finally, my lack of a lunch sack.

Sean's expression clouds over and I can practically read his mind: He thinks that after I said no to him, I went all blowout fabulous to go to lunch with...

David.

Flipping.

Chancellor.

In protest, I step my turquoise boots a foot away from David. It's almost a jump, really. Both boys look at me, confused. Then Sean's eyes narrow a little.

"Guess I'll see you later," he says to me. And then he and his friends are gone.

"What's with him?" David steps in front of me and opens the door just like Sean did the first day I met him, but the gesture seems too obvious this time.

"I don't know," I say, passing through. "Thanks."

Once we're inside, David looks like he's going to say something else, but I cut him off. "Well, have a good lunch."

I rush away, and with every step in the direction of my locker, I feel the pull of the student lot. I want to flip around and explain things to Sean, but I don't, because what would I say? "Don't worry, Sean, David doesn't like me, me; he likes the *other* me?"

Sure, Lizzie, that's a splendid idea.

It's almost painful, but I fake a migraine in dance and watch from the sidelines instead. When Ella was spinning from chatting last night with Dave, I convinced her to flat iron her curls today. It's vain, but I don't want to mess up my hair, particularly since Sean seems to be mad. I need all the ammo I can get. So I don't participate, but all through dance, I tap my boots to the music and visualize myself doing the moves.

When the bell rings, I spring up and leave; less than five minutes later, I'm one of four other students already seated in creative writing. I pull out my Spanish textbook and start my homework to take my mind off waiting for Sean. Second translation in, there he is.

"Hey," he says as he slides into his seat. He faces front instead of turning around for a pre-class chat. Just when I'm going to tap him on the shoulder, Natasha with the short blond hair and big boobs across the aisle speaks to him.

"Hi, Sean," she says in a sultry tone that makes me want to hurl.

"Hey, Natasha," he says. "How's it going?"

"I'm good. You?"

"I'm okay," Sean says. There's a little bite to his words; Natasha must hear it, too, because when her friend starts talking about some surfer, she turns away from Sean.

I lean forward and speak quietly to the back of his right shoulder. "Is everything okay?"

He inches his head to the right and laughs in one forced exhale through his nose. I want to kick the back of his chair to make him turn all the way around and look at me. I check to make sure Mr. Ames is still milling around in the hallway, then lean forward and try again.

"Sean," I say, a bit more forcefully. Finally—maybe because he's starting to get that I won't stop if he doesn't— he turns in his chair. His light brown eyes are cold.

"Nice lunch?" he asks, still holding my stare. Oddly, warmth spreads through my midsection because Sean's jealous. It's confirmation: He likes me, too.

"Yeah...at home," I say, smiling. "Dave and I just walked in at the same time; he had all that food for the debate team."

Sean's eyes stay on mine, so I see them soften. The corners of his lips turn up just a little, right before Mr. Ames comes into the classroom.

"Oh," he says sheepishly before facing front. I fight back a smile.

"How's everyone doing today?" Mr. Ames asks, taking his spot at the podium. A few people mutter weak responses; he turns to write on the white board.

"I really did have other plans," I whisper to Sean's shoulder. "But I wanted to go to lunch with you."

"Me, too," Sean whispers before turning and zapping me once with those eyes of his, leaving me wired the rest of class.

"We're out of soda," I say to Ella, my face in the refrigerator. She's over near the pantry digging for after-dinner snacks, tossing out pretzels and granola bars and Pirate's Booty. Betsey comes in wearing jammies, her hair pulled back and her face scrubbed clean: She always changes quickly after work.

"No way," Bet says, walking over to check the fridge I've just vacated, which bugs me like a gnat charging my face.

"I just said there wasn't any."

Bet shuts the refrigerator door and rolls her eyes at me. "Sometimes you miss things."

"Go get some!" Ella whines to anyone who will listen. "There's no way I can stay up to finish my paper without a Diet."

"You go get some," Betsey says. "I just got home."

They both look at me; I look down at myself. I'm in jeans and a T-shirt. I frown at them.

"But you're still dressed," Ella protests the protest that I didn't even have to vocalize. "Just go to the Quick Mart. It'll take like five seconds."

"Get some ice cream, too," Bet adds, smiling because she knows I'll cave.

"Fine," I say, sighing and leaving the room. I pull on the coat and grab the keys, then check the wallet. "There's no money in here," I shout from the entryway.

"Sorry!" Bet shouts back. "I bought dinner out. Go to the ATM."

Wanting to go stalk Facebook instead of spending time driving around San Diego in search of diet soda and ice cream, I opt for thievery instead. I clomp into Mom's first-floor office, then open the drawer where she keeps a small amount of money for emergencies in a pretty little box. It has a bunch of passwords written on a yellow sticky note taped to the outside. *Real secure, Mom.* I take forty dollars and close the lid and the drawer, then for some reason, I peek in the others.

There's nothing inside but meticulously straightened office supplies, medical files for each of us, and a stack of bank statements from Wyoming. I know what they are—and why they're from Wyoming, of all places—but something makes me reach out and grab the one on the top. I'm curious. But then Ella startles me with her shouts from the kitchen.

"Hurry up! I need fuel!"

I sigh loudly, then replace the statement and shut the open desk drawers. I flip off the light, leaving Mom's office as I found it, minus two crisp twenty-dollar bills.

six

Loud voices in the kitchen wake me up earlier than usual on Saturday morning. I roll out of bed and leave my room to investigate; Ella's in the hall with crazy hair and an even crazier expression.

"What's going on?" she asks. I listen and hear that Mom and Betsey are in a heated discussion. Mom says something about dating, and I'm jolted into action, grabbing Ella's hand and pulling her down the hallway and the stairs.

"—looks bad. It makes us look like a loser," Bet says as we walk into the kitchen. She's standing near the island in striped PJ bottoms and a faded T-shirt, arms folded defensively over her chest.

"I'm sure that's an exaggeration," Mom says, frowning

from her seat at the table in the breakfast nook. She glances at me and Ella. "Good morning," she says in a clipped tone.

"Morning," we mutter in unison. Ella blocks the doorway, curious, but I shove her through and we start making breakfast. Ella gets two mugs from the cabinet and pours coffee from the pot, then puts three sugars in each on autopilot. She hands me mine; I take a sip before busying myself with toast.

"Let's discuss it some other time," Mom says to Betsey. Betsey snorts.

"No," Bet says, "let's discuss it now. We're seventeen years old! We should be allowed to date!"

"You're *sixteen*," Mom says.

"Sixteen and a half," Bet mutters. "Actually sixteen and three quarters."

"You're asking if we can *date?*" Ella asks excitedly, getting it now.

"Yeah, but apparently, Mom thinks we still like My Little Pony more than boys or something," Betsey says.

"Betsey, I've had enough of your attitude," Mom says. "You know perfectly well why dating is a risk...to all of us."

"Not if we're careful," I say evenly, knowing and trying to wordlessly remind Betsey that calm is a better approach with Mom. I lean against the counter in a disarming stance. "If we're careful, hanging out with a guy is just like going to night class."

"I think you're too young," Mom says again, but her

voice is definitely softer this time. I can sense her walls weakening. Ella leans into the counter, too, and Bet sits down at the table with Mom, pulling her right leg up under her. They get it.

"We're old enough to wait tables," I say carefully.

"And drive," Ella adds, her tone measured.

"And fly an airplane, at least as a student flier," Bet jokes. We all look at her like she's lost it. "What?" she says, laughing. "It looks fun!"

"I think the point we're trying to make is that we're growing up, Mom," I say, looking her right in the brown eyes that I always felt I inherited despite being made from someone else's DNA. "We're not little girls anymore."

My words hang in the air until Mom sighs them away. She stands up and moves some plates to the sink, not talking while she does it. It's tense in the room, but I do my best to remain unruffled—I know it's helping Betsey stay that way, too.

Finally, Mom speaks. "There would be several non-negotiable conditions," she says slowly. I don't want to send her back to "no," but silly Ella rushes over and hugs Mom's shoulders. Mom hugs back for a moment, then gently pries Ella's arms loose. "I haven't agreed yet," she says.

"Let her talk," I say to Ella; she nods.

"What are the conditions?" Betsey asks, slouching lower into her chair and picking at a freezer waffle on a serving dish.

"Well," Mom says, stalling like she's making up rules on the fly. "The necklace must be worn at all times, as usual."

We all agree; that's a given.

"You'll have a curfew of ten o'clock and—"

"Uh, Mom?" I interrupt. "That's a little early, don't you think?"

"Eighth graders stay out later than that," Betsey says.

"Seriously," Ella adds, and she does look pretty serious about it.

"Fine," Mom says. "Eleven."

I bite my cheek to keep from smiling like I've been asked to appear on a dancing reality show.

But then Mom's eyes cloud over. "I'm not sure what to do about..." Her words trail off and she twists her face in that way that she does when she's considering something. I want to ask what she means, but I'm afraid to say anything. "Everyone thinks there's only one Elizabeth, so obviously you can only date one boy. I'm not sure how to make it fair."

"Straws?" Betsey offers. "Like our rooms?"

"This is a little more important than bedroom assignments," Mom says, frowning. "I don't know. Maybe it's all just too complicated. Maybe you should wait another—"

"You pick the guy," Betsey blurts out. Ella and I both look at her, eyes wide with surprise.

"You can't be serious," I say to her.

"Actually, it's a good idea," Mom says. "Who you date matters. We don't want anyone you're associated with drawing attention to our situation. I think Betsey's suggestion is a great one."

"But how would that even work?" Ella says. She looks as sick as I feel. Secrets or not, it seems wrong not to be able to just date who I want.

"Hmm . . . I guess you three can each pick a boy, and tell me a little about him, and then I'll take a day or two to decide," she says, smiling like it's the most natural thing in the world. "Fair?"

Not at all.

No one answers, so Mom continues. "Let me know when you've all figured out who you'd like to submit."

"David Chancellor," Ella blurts out.

Mom stifles a laugh. "Well, then," she says, walking back to the table and grabbing the pencil she'd probably been using for the crossword. She writes David's name on a corner of the newspaper.

"Lizzie?" she asks, looking up at me.

"Sean Kelly," I say, and despite the ridiculousness of the situation, I smile at just the sound of his name. She narrows her eyes and smiles a little, too, then writes. When she's finished, she looks up at Betsey.

"And you?"

Betsey shakes her head. "I forfeit," she says with a satisfied smirk on her face. "Better chances for the ones who actually like someone." She doesn't meet my gaze.

"Sometimes I don't understand you at all," Mom mutters to Betsey. She starts cleaning again with purpose.

Ella sits down to eat, but before I join her, I look at Betsey. I know that all of it, from bringing up dating in the first place to the "you pick" thing to keep Mom from throwing out the idea altogether, was all for me.

Thanks, I think at her. She smiles like she heard me.

seven

Sunday, Mom decides that she wants to go to the book-store with her daughter, and it happens to be afternoon, so I'm the one dragged along. Normally, I'm all for leaving the house, and bookstores are among my favorite places to be. But my mind's on Sean, and frankly, all I really want to do is listen to sappy songs and think about him.

"How are you, Lizzie?" Mom asks in that fully loaded way of hers as we drive through the gate in the luxury sedan she bought when we moved here.

"This car smells like Band-Aids," I say. "It always has."

Mom looks at me funny. "Are you dodging my question?"

"I'm fine," I say, looking out the window. "Have you decided about the dating thing yet?"

"Not yet," she says quietly. "Do you want to talk about it at all?"

And say what? Pick me! Pick me!

"No."

"Who's Sean?" she asks.

"I just said I don't want to talk about it."

She gives me a look, so I give in.

"Fine. He's a guy in my creative writing class." I have to turn my head so far to the right it hurts and bite the inside of my cheek to keep from grinning.

"I see," Mom says, reaching over to turn down the air-conditioning. She's always cold. "What else?"

I consider telling her about Sean's photography. His laid-back style. His general awesomeness. Instead, I say simply, "Nothing."

We ride in silence for a few seconds, and I start thinking about how I really should be campaigning for Sean when Ella's not around to do the same for Dave. But I don't want to have to campaign for the guy I like. I just want to see what happens. The whole thing is so unnatural and unfair and unrealistic and a million other un words that I wish I would've just stayed home.

We pull up to a red light and Mom looks at me, concerned. "Is everything okay?" The light turns green, so she's forced to look away, but that doesn't stop her from talking. "You've seemed sort of sulky lately."

"I'm not sulky," I snap. "I'm just...over it."

"Over what?"

Immediately, I want to take back what I said, not because I didn't mean it, but because I don't want to get into a big discussion about it. I think Mom believes that we're content or at least satisfied with the situation. And I guess until recently, we have been. I have been...maybe because I didn't know any better. But now I know things need to change...I just don't know how. And without knowing, now's not the time to open that can of catastrophe.

"Betsey keeps taking my clothes," I lie. "I'm so completely over it I could scream. She has no respect for my personal space. And it's not like she doesn't have the exact same outfits as I do. She says that her closet smells, but whatever, that's her problem."

"I'll talk to her," Mom says, holding back a laugh, which tells me that she believes what I said. I'm quiet the rest of the way to the bookstore.

Inside, we walk a few aisles together, then split up. I look at practically every cover and read every description on the paperback new releases table, then settle on a book I saw Alison reading before dance last week. When I'm finished, I meet up with Mom at the coffee corner.

"You're right, you know," Mom says after taking a sip of her latte.

"Of course I am," I joke. "But about what specifically?"

She laughs. "You're growing up. You're practically a

woman." She reaches over and brushes a piece of lint off my hoodie.

"Ew, Mom, don't talk about me being a woman in public," I say, which makes her chuckle again.

"Sorry, Elizabeth." She only calls me Elizabeth when we're out of the house together. "I'm just sentimental."

"It's okay. I get what you're saying."

I nod toward the door and Mom follows. As we walk into the bright sun, I'm happy to be spending time with her, and I even start to feel a little nostalgic. I think of the lime-green playhouse in Florida that she bought used and decorated with scrap wallpaper and carpeting. She'd fold herself in with all three of us so we could snuggle and read bedtime stories. She'd sing us this made-up song called "Three Little Birdies"; I always loved it.

On one of the walls, she hung labeled pictures, cut out of magazines and books, of far-off people and places—I think she wanted us to be worldly even though we never went anywhere. The thought of how hard Mom worked to make ours a happy home squeezes my heart. In this moment, I feel close to her again, just like we used to be.

Two hours later, I hate my mother with all the fiery passion I possess.

At dinner, she drops the bomb: We're approved to date David Chancellor. Apparently, she has a friend in the counselor's office at school and— Who really cares why or how? The bottom line is that on paper at least, David's better than Sean.

As Ella and Betsey ask logistical questions, like "Are we really going to split dating him or can Ella go out at night if there's a nighttime date?" I think of nothing but how Mom probably knew what her decision was going to be when she made me go to the bookstore today. Why did she even bother to ask about Sean if she was planning to nix my chances with him later?

In the midst of the conversation, I stand up and drop my full plate of pasta into the sink, then storm up to my room. No one stops me, and no one comes in the rest of the night.

Later, Sean unknowingly pours salt in the wound.

I think we should meet at halftime on Friday.

I stare at the Facebook instant message for a full minute, cycling through emotions. At first, I'm elated—he wants to meet up!—but then I'm heartbroken by the reality of my life. Nothing about this situation is even remotely fair. And although I should find some way to politely decline, I don't. In this moment, it's like I'm possessed by a regular girl: a girl whose mom doesn't dictate who she dates.

Oh, you do, huh?

I see that he's writing another message and wait nervously to read it.

Yep. I mean, you'll be cheering; I'll be taking pictures. Seems perfect.

It *is*, I message back, meaning it. It's a great idea; in

fact, it's the best I've heard all week. I add a smiley-face icon, thankful that Sean can't see my real face: red and blotchy from crying. Sighing a long, heavy sigh, I read:

So? You in?

I bite my lip, trying to think of an excuse. I know I can't commit to this. Mom was clear: It's Dave or no one. But beyond that, games are at night; Betsey would be the one to meet Sean. Agreeing to this is as pointless as wearing a raincoat in San Diego. But despite all that, the regular girl in me just wants to enjoy the moment.

I can't force my fingers to go near the n or the o. Instead, I type:

Maybe.

eight

Mom's leaving for work when I get home from school on Friday. We don't usually see each other in the afternoons—which has been a blessing this week—but there's no cheer practice since there's a game tonight.

"I left chicken and rice in the fridge for supper," she says when I walk into the kitchen.

"Why can't you just say 'dinner' like normal people?" I ask, hearing the ridiculousness of my gripe. "And I hate chicken," I add, which is among the most untrue statements ever uttered. But I'm still mad at her, and I'm boycotting chicken to prove it. Or at least I'm telling her I am; you never know what'll happen when dinnertime rolls around.

Not wanting to see her stupid face, I go upstairs to my

room and slam the door. I fall onto the bed and scream into the pillow. This week has been beyond annoying. Not only have I been tortured by seeing Sean and his wanting-to-hang-out self, but Ella wasted no time setting something up with Dave. They went out on a coffee date, and unfortunately, it went well.

At least I'm not the one who has to hang out with the guy.

Since even Mom was grossed out by the idea of three girls dating the same person at once—even if no one else knows we're three—it was decided that Ella's the one who's going to actually do the dating. I mean, I still have to be polite to Dave at school, but Ella's in charge of the rest. What that means—what's making me hibernate in the caves of my pillow right now—is that all this was for nothing . . . at least from my perspective. Ultimately, Ella won big—getting closer to a life of her own—and I just flat-out lost.

I'm still lying facedown on my bed when Ella comes in a while later. She's talking on the phone, and at first, I think she's going to rub my nose in her "win."

"Leave me alone," I mutter into my pillow.

"Bet wants to talk to you," she says, tapping me on the arm with the cordless. Glad that it's Betsey, I reach out and take it.

"Where are you?" I ask.

"Picking up my uniform from the dry cleaner," Bet says. "Geez, you sound like crap."

"Thanks," I say. "I'm fine." From the foot of my bed, Ella gives me a knowing look. "I'll be fine," I add.

"El said you told her that Sean asked you to meet at the game."

"Yeah." The phone is uncomfortably smashed into my cheek, but I don't have the will to lift my head and ease my own pain.

"Why didn't you tell me?" she asks, and I can tell from her voice that she feels a little hurt that I didn't share the story with her, too.

"Sorry." *Wow, I really do sound like crap.*

"It's okay," Betsey says. "Let me talk to Ella again for a quick sec." Glad to be off the hook, I hand Ella the phone, then drop my face back into the pillow. I listen to Ella's end of the conversation.

"Hi.

"I know.

"*I know.*

"What do you mean?

"Are you being serious right now?

"Yes, of course, but . . .

"She might. And then we'd all be dead.

"I don't know, B.

"Ugh . . . I just don't know.

"Maybe.

"Okay, fine, she would.

"Fine. But if she gets pissed, I'm going to burn your Birkenstocks."

Ella laughs and I can hear Betsey laughing on the other end of the line.

"Okay, sounds good. Don't forget to check the stain on my blue shirt before you pay, okay?

"I know, but last time they didn't—

"Betsey, just do it!"

She listens for a long moment and then sighs.

"I know, I know.

"Yeah, I'll tell her.

"Okay, bye."

Ella disconnects the phone and I feel it thump onto the middle of the bed. She doesn't say anything for so long that I finally pull up my head and look at her. She's got her arms crossed over her chest and she's staring at me with pity and a plan in her eyes.

"What's going on?" I ask.

"You're doing evening tonight," she says, matter-of-fact.

I bolt up to sitting, eyes wide. "What?"

"You heard me."

"Yes, but WHAT?" I say. "You're not saying what I think you're saying . . . are you?"

"She . . . we . . . feel really badly that you're not getting your shot with Sean," Ella says softly. "We want you to have this one night. So yeah, I'm saying what you think I'm saying."

My heart pounds hard and fast in my chest. "We're doing a switch."

* * *

We used to try to trick Mom a lot when we were little. I'd wear Betsey's favorite T-shirt or Ella would ask for my favorite food for dinner, just to see if she'd be able to tell. She always saw through our makeshift disguises, but we loved it. It was a game, and every time we were called out, we'd launch into a giggle fit cubed, then start plotting our next attempt. But as we got older, particularly when we were made to live as one person, silly switches became less fun.

Nervous as I am about Mom finding out, tonight feels fun again.

I make my way to City Stadium in the dying daylight. At one point, on a particularly dark stretch of road, a passing car flashes its lights at me and I realize that my headlights are off. I flip them on, and driving becomes significantly easier.

When I arrive, I walk with my chin up like I know where I'm going through the lot, then head under the bleachers toward the field. I try not to make it obvious that I'm reading the signs; thankfully, there are many, and they are bold. I turn and make my way down a long tunnel behind several football players. I scan to confirm that none of them is David.

When I emerge from the darkness, my senses come to life. Massive lights shine so brightly that they make the green grass seem fake. I look down at my yellow and black uniform and practically need sunglasses it's so vibrant. I suck in my breath and get high on the fresh air and the scent of just-clipped grass. I listen to the sound of hard plastic hitting hard plastic, the grunts of boys warming up, instruments being tuned. I shiver when a breeze winds around my bare legs like a kitten's tail. I look up to the first few stars already shimmering in the darkening sky even though there's a glow of daylight peeking through. I feel overwhelmed, and without warning, tears pop into my eyes.

I'm out at night.

"Elizabeth!" someone calls. "Elizabeth! Over here!"

I see Grayson waving at me, with Morgan, Jane, Natalie, and a few others smiling behind her. I'm neither first nor last to arrive: just how I like it. I smile and wave back, then work my way down the ramp to meet up with the girls. I look around for Sean, but he's nowhere to be found.

"This is amazing," I say to Grayson when I join her and the others on the sidelines. She nods, but looks confused: She's been here before and assumes that I have, too. Except that I haven't—Betsey has. Thankfully, she doesn't point out my weirdness.

Isla and several other squad members arrive. We start stretching, and more girls appear from the tunnel. Soon, we're fifteen strong and the bleachers are filling up and the players head into their respective locker rooms to get pumped for the game of the year, against Woodbury's biggest rival. According to Grayson, this game is even bigger than Homecoming.

"Guys, line up!" she shouts. "Let's get the crowd going."

I move to the center row with the four other medium-height girls and make sure I'm staggered to the right of short Isla in front of me. I know tall Simone behind me will do the same. The goal is for everyone to be visible from the student section.

Grayson begins by shouting, "Ready? Okay!" Then everyone joins in.

Bang, bang, choo-choo train!

Come on, Woodchucks, do your thang . . .

The words are completely humiliating, but the moves are a little like jazz, so I zone out and pretend I'm on the dance team instead. Except there is no dance team. The cheer is an easy one consisting of simple clapping, kicking, and jumping—no lifts—so I just go with it and even add an extra high kick at the end.

Grayson calls out, "Spirit!"

We've got spirit, yes, we do!

We've got spirit, how 'bout you?

The growing crowd yells back at us. Yep, they've got spirit. The starter cheers go on for a while until the bleachers are packed and the band starts playing. That's when Grayson brings out the big guns, like "Launcher!" and "Human Cannonball!"

Thankfully, it's only the short girls in row one who get tossed up in the air. But I swear, every time gravity takes over and Isla or Jane or Maya drops back down, I hold my breath until she's on solid ground again. After "Fireball," I turn to see what's happening on the field.

Sean is standing on the edge of center field, pointing a massive camera right at me. I tilt my head and give him a half smile, almost hearing the shutter go click. Then I turn away with a little head shake. I move back into formation and refocus on cheering so I don't get booted in the face. I do my best not to gawk at him the rest of the game, but there's rarely a moment I'm not aware of where he is.

I can't say that I'm a huge football fan, but I do manage to get into the action. In fact, I'm so caught up in the final play before halftime that when the whistle blows, I get that little start you do when you forget and then remember something exciting.

Sounds bombard me: The announcer booms about the marching band's halftime performance. Grayson shouts, "Meet back in twenty!" Morgan squeals about how some guy she likes looks in his uniform. But I'm focused. In my bubble, I watch Sean pack up his camera equipment and stow it in one of the locked bins under the bleachers.

The squad scatters like marbles and I take off, too, having to check myself so I don't run to the south entrance. Sean's closer to that end of the field than I am; I can see him moving in the direction of our meeting place before hoards of snack-stalkers surrounding the concession stands block my view.

I am a ball of nerves as I zoom down the right side of the rotunda. Most people are sauntering straight down the middle, happily bottlenecking the walkway as they chat about plays and passes. I can feel the precious seconds floating away like dead leaves in late fall. Finally, when I break through a blockade of dawdlers and reach our meeting point, I find Sean leaning on the left wall, looking out toward the parking lot.

I stop to catch my breath.

He looks over and smiles like sunshine.

Slowly, I close the gap between us.

"Hi," he says quietly.

"Hi."

"How much time do we have?"

Realizing that I left my cell in my coat under the bleachers, I ask, "What time is it?"

Sean pulls out his cell, taps it on, and shows it to me. The picture on the screen is a rusty old mailbox. I note the time.

"Eighteen minutes," I say.

"Then let's go." Sean grabs one of my cold hands and guides me outside. It's the first time he's held my hand, but it isn't awkward at all—it feels completely natural, like we've done it a thousand times before.

He steers us to the right around the outside of the stadium. I hadn't realized it before, but on this side the arena is built into a small hill. I let Sean lead me up in silence, feeling more alive than I have in a while. I admire the view even before we've reached the peak, but when we're standing on top of the world, looking down at the ant-sized people, I sigh.

"We're outside the light," I say. I mean it literally—the

field lights don't touch us here—but it sounds bigger than that.

"Yeah," Sean agrees, and I wonder how he means it. He turns to face me.

"So, you said in class your mom's pretty strict," he says. I nod. "Then how do we see each other?"

His directness forces a smile out of me. "I don't know," I say quietly. "I guess just at school."

"Not good enough."

I look down and he bends a little so he can see into my eyes. He's so tall; I love how tall he is.

"I like you, Elizabeth," he says, his voice steady. Warmth moves through me; I look away for a second. "We barely know each other, but I feel like we do, you know? That sounds so messed up, but—"

"No, I get it," I say. "I feel the same way."

A breeze blows my hair into my face and I shake it away. Looking at Sean, I see his happiness—to him this is obviously the beginning of something. But to me, everything about this night—from the stars to the colors to the rock anthem on the sound system now that the band is done to the perfect feeling in my low belly—is nothing but tomorrow's memory. It's nothing but what could have been.

It's nothing.

"I'm glad you feel the same way," Sean says, straightening up and glancing down at the field. "Now we just have to figure out how we can hang out." He squeezes my hand, and then, when I don't offer a solution, changes the subject. "I got a great picture of you tonight."

"I saw your pictures on Facebook," I say. Then I remember... "Did you go out with Grayson?" I ask.

"Gray?" Sean says, surprised. "No, no. We're just friends. We've lived across the street from each other since middle school."

I nod, then look down at the field; a few cheerleaders are already returning to our spot. I feel my twenty-minute date slipping away, and with it, all hope of having anything with Sean.

"It's almost over," I say sadly.

Sean looks at me, concerned. He can hear it in my voice. Maybe he does know me after all.

"What do you—"

"Sean?"

"Yeah?"

"Kiss me."

He looks surprised, but I stand strong instead of shrinking. I might be imagining it, but I think I feel Ella and Betsey supporting me. Pushing me forward. For the first time, I feel entitled—I've gone along with Mom's plan for seven years without stepping out of line. Now, if she tells me I can't date Sean—if this is really my one chance—I'm damn well taking it.

Sean doesn't say anything else. He takes a step toward me and puts one palm on my jawbone. He rubs my cheek with his thumb, then bends slightly and presses his warm lips to mine. We stay like that a moment, barely touching, barely breathing. Then he tilts his head and wraps his other hand around my back and our mouths open in unison and we kiss like a perfect first kiss should be. When he pulls away just a few inches and looks into my eyes, I grab a fistful of his sweatshirt so he won't go yet. I realize that his left hand is still clutching my low back. He doesn't want me to move, either.

Standing there under the brilliant sky, just out of reach of the field's floodlights, I am afraid that I'll never have anything like this again. I feel tears fill my eyes. Sean doesn't ask what's wrong; he doesn't even look surprised. He just wipes away what falls and kisses my tear tracks.

"We should go back," I whisper.

He nods. "Can I call you tonight after the game?"

"I don't know," I say honestly. Mom shouldn't be home, but sometimes she does the unexpected.

I can feel the questions radiating from him, but he doesn't ask anything. He just takes my hand and leads me back toward the entrance. But before we step out of the darkness, he turns quickly and kisses me again. Our lips are closed, but he presses into me so hard I have to put a hand on the wall to steady myself. He steps back and holds my gaze.

"I feel like..." I begin, trailing off because I'm not sure what I want to say. Instead, I plant my hand on his chest, right over his heart. He lets it stay there a moment, then pries it away and kisses my palm.

"Me, too," he says, turning to go.

"Sean?"

"Yeah?" He looks at me expectantly, and it makes me feel equal parts elated and crushed. Right now, I'm not sure whether having just a taste of him was worth it. And yet, even if it's a bad idea, I give him just a little bit more.

"You can call me Lizzie."

nine

It's eleven.

It's midnight.

It's two in the morning.

My chest is caving in on itself, folding in half and half again. Part of me—the part that keeps replaying the feel of Sean's lips on mine—is boiling over with happiness. That part is busying my wakeful brain with a movie montage of romantic times to come. That part is picking out prom dresses a season too early and whispering our names together to see whether it sounds better with his first or mine and wishing that he would've called even though I was so weird when he asked if he could.

But the other part of my brain is butting in, callously

reminding me of how much Sean and I aren't really together. How, unless things change, we won't ever be. Elizabeth Best is dating David Chancellor, and that's all there is to it. There's no Sean and Lizzie, or Lizzie and Sean: There's only David and Elizabeth. That's the part that keeps me up until three, tossing and turning, trying to find a comfortable position in bed.

But my heart hurts no matter which side I'm on.

When the sound of the vacuum wakes me up at seven, I roar out of bed from the wrong side. "Seriously?" I shout at Ella over the noise. "It's *way* too early for this!"

"Mom's in one of her cleaning frenzies," she shouts back. "We've all got lists of chores. I wanted to get mine done early."

"Agh!" I shout at her, even though it's not her fault. Every once in a while, when Mom's stressed about something, she turns into a Clean Bot. She assigns us things to do around the house, which really sucks, but I guess tidying up is how she deals. I'd wonder what set her off this time if I weren't so preoccupied by my own misery and tired from only a few hours of sleep. I stomp downstairs, thinking of nothing but Sean and how unfair everything is. I can't even be happy about my first kiss—about the fact that it was *awesome*—because my mom won't let me pursue it.

"I can see that you're in a good mood today," Mom says sarcastically the moment I walk into the kitchen. I almost gag from the smell of bleach.

"I'm fine," I mutter.

"Is this still about the boy?" Mom asks, wiping her forehead with the back of her gloved hand. The fact that she seems to think I should already be over it tells me that she doesn't believe my feelings are true.

"Whatever," I say, leaving the room, because I'd rather starve than be around her right now. This must really annoy her, because she follows me, sponge in hand.

"Lizzie," she says, "wait." I keep walking. "Elizabeth!" she says forcefully. "Stop." I don't. "Stop walking right this second!" Rattled by the rage in her voice, I freeze, then turn around. My mom takes a deep breath.

"We need to talk about this."

"Will it change anything?" I ask. "Will talking make it so I can hang out with the guy I like instead of the one Ella does?" The vacuum's off now; I hear the floor creak upstairs. I know they're listening.

Mom looks down and away, then back at me. "Lizzie," she says, "you wanted to date. You knew it'd be possible that you'd have to go along with dating David. You accepted those terms."

I roll my eyes at her formal language. "Yeah, great, I accepted those terms," I say. "Fine, Mom. Whatever. Just let me go upstairs and Cinderella the day away. Just leave me alone."

My mom looks stunned at first, then there's a fire in her eyes like I've never seen, not even when Betsey got a three-hundred-dollar speeding ticket. I wonder: Is this the first time we've ever had a real fight?

"Elizabeth Best, cut the attitude right now. In life, we make choices, and then we live with them. You said you're growing up, now start acting like it. Live with the choice you made."

Something snaps inside me, and suddenly, my mom's feelings and future are not my priority. Maybe for the first time, I only care about me.

"The choice I made?" I shout, fuming. "Was it my choice to be stolen from some lab? Was it my choice to run? Was it my choice to live as a third of a person? No! All of those were *your* choices, not mine!"

My mom's jaw tightens as she clearly tries to compose herself.

"I've told you this a thousand times," she says through clenched teeth, "but the people who paid us to create you only wanted one. The *best* one. They wanted the perfect baby, and the other two—who were not as perfect—would've been..." Her words trail off. "I had to take you. I had to do it." Mom lifts her chin a little, resolute.

She's told us the story a lot, but only since we moved to California. Before then, it was all innocence and bliss. After we fled Florida, she told us about her work at the genetics lab that was secretly cloning humans while the rest of the world was getting excited about a cloned sheep. She told us about her boss, Dr. Jovovich, who was in on the plan to steal us. She showed us the newspaper reports from when his practice was exposed and he was publicly taken to jail in handcuffs—when, under oath, he admitted that we just might exist.

When everything changed.

"Yes, you're such a martyr," I say sarcastically. "You implanted the embryos into your womb like the Virgin Mary of Science and gave up your whole life to raise us. Well, thanks. I mean, living a third of a life is almost as good as having a real one."

My mom looks so floored by what's flying out of my mouth that for a blink I think I'm done. But then, the unfairness of Sean driving me, I throw one final insult at her.

"I'm not even sure why you bothered. You're not even our real mom. You should have just left the un-best of us to die."

I turn and go back upstairs, running by Ella and Betsey and their open mouths on the way to my room. To my bed. I'm shaking with the realization that I've just unlocked something better left shut tight. I've changed my relationship with my mother. And worse, I've never felt so unsure of who I am, which is pretty messed up coming from someone who's already broken in three pieces anyway.

After a few hours, the guilt is weighing me down to the point that I know I have to apologize. Even though I'm mad at Mom for not letting me date Sean, what I said was horrible. And ultimately, I know that the way back to normal—to Ella, Betsey, and I living as three people instead of one—is first a truce, and then, eventually, a conversation. But everything starts with me saying I'm sorry.

I leave my room to find her, but when I go downstairs, she's not around.

"She just left," Betsey says, looking at me disappointedly. "Like, just right now."

"Where's she going?" I ask.

Betsey shrugs. "Running errands before work."

"I need to talk to her," I say, knowing that the longer it takes to apologize, the worse it'll be. "I'm going after her."

I rush to the entryway and shove my feet into whatever shoes are there, then grab the keys and run out of the house. I jump into the car and race up the driveway, tapping my fingers on the steering wheel while I wait for the painfully slow gate to open.

"Come on!" I shout at it.

Once I'm through, I pull up to the busy street and look both ways: I can see Mom stopped at the light down the hill to the left. I wait for some cars to pass, then turn and quickly move into the same lane she's in. About six cars behind because no one will let me pass, I follow her down the hill and through town, past the mail place where she has her PO box, the drugstore where she buys her vitamins, and the bulk supermarket where she stocks up on stuff for the house. I follow her until we pass everything familiar.

Then I start to get curious.

I'm still three cars back when Mom pulls into a parking lot next to a duplex that's been converted to office space. Not wanting her to see me, I drive past and park a little way down the street. I watch as she walks up the steps to the office front door. Then, instead of just going inside or knocking, like you would with an open business, Mom pulls out a key and unlocks the door herself.

"What is this place?" I ask aloud.

As I'm musing to myself about why an ER doctor needs a private office, Mom emerges, locks the door, and gets in her car and drives away. I don't follow: I drive around the block and park in the space she just vacated. I try the door, and attempt to see into a window, but everything's locked and dark. I walk around the side, searching for another way in, but there's nothing. Completely confused—apology forgotten—I return to the sedan and drive home wondering. I mean, maybe it's nothing.

But in this strange life I lead, you never know.

Maybe it's something, instead.

ten

I wake up completely focused on and unsettled by the possibility of Mom having secrets—and what they could be. Then my emotions flip like a switch and I turn pure mad when I remember that it's Sunday: the day I get to go to a movie with a guy I don't even like, thanks to Ella's clumsiness and a stupid short straw.

Most inconveniently, Ella twisted her ankle last night. She was cagey about it, but Betsey told me she'd been dancing around her room, trying on outfits, and she tripped over a pair of shoes. Mom said it looked fine but that Ella needed to stay off it for a day...maybe two days. Normal teens would go to the movie anyway, hobbling if they had to, to spend time with their crush. But in our house, if you're limping or coughing, you're housebound. It's too hard to fake someone else's affliction, and god forbid the school nurse would want to take a look.

When Dave rings the buzzer on the gate one minute early, I push the button to let him through and then peer out the window as he navigates the drive in a different gleaming Lexus from the one I saw him driving at school. *Does he live on a Lexus farm?* The car and the whole thing make me cringe, but knowing how Ella must feel about me going on *her* date, I vow to be nice and try to have a good time. At least I get to see a movie.

"Hi, Dave," I say sweetly when I open the door.

"Hi, Elizabeth," he says, eyeing my casual wrap dress, pausing a little too long at the neckline. "Nice threads."

"Thanks," I say, pulling on a jacket and buttoning it up to the top. I force myself to notice what he's wearing: a button-down with checkered Vans and jeans. I have to admit, he doesn't look bad, either, but I hold in the thought.

"Ready to roll?" he asks, shifting awkwardly, like maybe underneath it all, he's nervous. Honestly, it makes me warm to him a bit.

"Um . . . my mom wants to meet you. Is that okay?"

"Of course," Dave says easily. "Parents love me." I sigh too quietly for him to notice: Apparently that glimmer of sweet nervousness has been replaced by cockiness.

Despite the fact that the last time we spoke we were screaming at each other, Mom is inquisitive but friendly;

despite the fact that I saw her at a secret office, I'm polite back. Thankfully, she doesn't keep us too long: We're out of the house less than five minutes later.

Beyond her reach and anger and secrets, I relax on the way to the multiplex. Dave isn't my style, but he's okay... as a friend.

"Nice car," I say as I lean back in the passenger seat.

"Yeah," Dave says. "My dad let me borrow it."

"Don't you have one just like it?"

"Mine's used, but yes," Dave says, glancing at me with a smile that I'm sure makes some girls swoon. "I drive it to and from practice and sometimes some of the other guys get rides. It smells like french fries and sweaty socks."

"Thanks for saving me from that, Dave's dad."

"Should we call him?" Dave jokes. "You two can have a little chat."

"Oh, totally," I say. "In fact, why don't we just invite him along?"

We both laugh that polite sort of laughter that happens when you don't know someone well, and when it's over, when no one has anything else to say about Dave's dad, the car falls silent. It lasts only a moment before Dave reaches over and plugs in his iPod. He scrolls through and selects a playlist; the first song is a slowed-down remake of a hip-hop classic. He looks at me expectantly, like I'm going to start singing or something.

"What?" I ask, my pulse quickening a bit. This is where stepping into someone else's relationship gets dicey.

"I found it," he says, nodding to the iPod.

"Your iPod?" I ask, smiling in case I'm way off base—maybe he'll think I'm joking.

"Funny," he says. "No, the *song*."

"Oh!" I say, pretending to remember a conversation that Ella failed to mention. I'm mad for a second until I remember that she *did* tell me a lot—obviously it's hard to remember every word she's uttered to Dave and vice versa. "Yes, you did."

"See? I told you it was good. Pretty killer, right?"

"The killer-est." In my opinion, the original is much better, but I can see Ella liking this one.

"It reminds me of you," Dave says, which reminds me of Sean. Those same words from Sean's lips would give me shivers; from Dave, it's a line. How many songs have been dedicated to how many girls in this pristine Lexus?

"That's sweet," I say, looking out the window. I try to think of something else to talk about.

"San Diego is so much better than Florida," I say out of nowhere.

"I forget which city you said you lived in," Dave says as he makes a left; I can see the theater down on the right. "Were you close to Miami?"

"Unfortunately not." I flash back to the one-story house outside of Clearwater where I spent most of my young life. "We lived in a small town you've never heard of. Lots of alligators and lawn flamingos."

"Alligators? Serious?"

"Dead. There was one in our front yard once. Animal control in Florida is about a lot more than lost kitties."

"That's so badass," he says, nodding, then getting this faraway look like he's imagining himself wrestling an alligator with his bare hands. He pulls out of the quick daydream and adds, "But it's good that you moved...that you're here now. You're a nice distraction from Milo's sinuses in student government. Man, that guy would so get eaten by a gator."

I don't have first period with Dave now, but I did before the trig quiz and the switch, so I know who he's talking about. And I know he's being mean.

"Milo can't help his breathing problem," I say frankly. We're in the lot now, and Dave's searching for a spot; he's focused on turning into one that's too small for the car.

"He sounds like a pig," Dave says distractedly.

"He does not," I say, shaking my head. Dave turns off the car and looks at me, and it's like a lightbulb goes on in his head. He backpedals.

"Naw, I'm just kidding," he says. "Milo's a good guy. I know he can't help it. Did you know he's getting an operation to fix it?"

"Really?"

I want him to tell me about how he and Milo go way back. I want him to tell me that they hang out sometimes, and that's how Dave knows about the operation. I want him to redeem himself, because as much as I don't like him, Ella does. And I don't want her to like a bully.

Instead, Dave just nods, then opens his door. "You ready?" he asks.

No, I think. But I say . . .

"Can't wait."

Dave lets me pick the movie; I go for the expected romantic comedy. I could've acted cool by choosing the sci-fi thriller or the indie about the druggie race-car driver, but I haven't seen anything in the theater in over a year and I'm taking the opportunity to girl out a little.

We sit in the middle, just off the left aisle, and Dave immediately stands again to go buy snacks. I turn off my ringtone, then alternate between rocking preshow trivia and watching the other moviegoers choose their seats. There are couples of all ages, from the cutest old man and woman I've ever seen to parents with an afternoon baby-sitter to a pair of tweeners who probably got dropped off at the mall by one of their moms. There's a four-pack of girls from school; I've seen them around, but I don't know any of their names. One of them keeps turning around and looking at me, probably because I'm with Dave, who everyone seems to know. And there's one scruffy-looking guy sitting alone who makes me nervous until an even scruffier-looking woman sits down next to him.

There's someone for everyone, I think to myself as Dave reappears.

"Here you go," he says too loudly for the quiet theater.

"Thanks," I say, taking my frozen Junior Mints and

water from his outstretched hands. I rip open the candy box and start munching.

Dave eats some of his popcorn and we don't talk for a few minutes. I wish the movie would start so the silence wouldn't seem so obvious. Instead, Dave clears his throat.

"So you live with just your mom, right?"

"Uh-huh," I say warily.

"What happened to your dad?" he asks, catching me off guard. It seems surprisingly bold until I remember that he and Ella have probably chatted about family before. Even still, I don't feel like making up a story when the truth is that I don't have a dad. The Original did—she had the happy family—but then she died and her parents contracted my mom's lab to bring her back from the dead, and our mom stole us and said it didn't work. End of story.

"Uh, he's not..." I begin, my voice trailing off because I'm not sure what to say. I don't want to lie, but I can't tell the truth. I try to think of something appropriately vague. Finally, I say, "I don't really know what happened to him. It's not something my mom talks about a lot."

"Oh, okay," he says, and I think I see a flicker of disappointment in his eyes. "I didn't mean to bring up a bad subject. Sorry."

"It's no big deal, I just don't know," I say. "It's sort of embarrassing."

"Sorry," Dave says again, looking embarrassed himself. It's amazing how he can go from looking like an overconfident ass to a sheepish kid in under ten minutes. He faces front toward the screen and eats a few handfuls of popcorn. I consider that I might be messing this up by being too...me.

What would Ella do?

"Thanks for bringing me," I say quietly as the preview-rating screen lights our faces green. I shove doubts about Dave from my mind and just smile.

Dave smiles back at me in a way that, for maybe the first time today, feels perfectly genuine. "No," he says, leaning in a little closer to me and lowering his voice to a more theater-appropriate volume, "thank you. You picked the movie I really wanted to see."

When the credits roll, Dave and I leave and go to the massive two-story bookstore and browse. I make a beeline to the music section; Dave follows. As we walk the aisles, he interviews me like he's a journalist. Ella warned me that he likes to play Twenty Questions.

"What's your middle name?"

"Violet."

"Pretty," he says, nodding his approval.

"When's your birthday?" he continues. "You know mine from that thing in government, but when it was your turn, the bell rang."

"January thirtieth," I say.

"That's coming up," he says. "Noted." He wiggles his eyebrows at me in this totally cheesy way that makes me want to frown; I force myself to smile. The questions continue. "Do you have any pets?"

"No, do you?" I ask, attempting to turn the tables.

"No," he says. "What's your favorite food?"

"Bacon."

This makes Dave laugh so loudly that people three aisles over turn to look. When it goes on for a few seconds, I start to feel like he's making fun of me.

"What?" I ask.

"Nothing," he says. "Bacon's just not...I meant more like your favorite kind of food."

"Any kind with bacon," I say before putting on earphones to sample a just-released CD. This forces Dave to stop with the questioning. I listen and watch him wander; he looks a little lost without me to talk to. As I'm trying to figure him out it hits me: He hasn't figured himself out yet. Trying to act casual, he strolls down a couple of aisles before he ends up near the stairs that lead to the second level. I watch him pause, turn, and gesture that he's going up, coincidentally to the beat of the song playing in my ears. I nod, then point to my ears to tell him I'm going to keep listening. When he disappears from view, I feel free: I hum along and tap my thumbs on the CD cover I'm holding. The title track ends and a ballad begins, and someone

95

taps on my shoulder. I turn around to find Sean in dark jeans and a black shirt, his hair wilder than usual. He looks at me excitedly; he's holding the same CD in his hands.

I rip the earphones from my ears.

"Hi!" I say, wide-eyed and smiling.

"Hi," he says back, looking almost as happy to see me as I am to see him. "It's good, isn't it?" he says, pointing to the CD case.

"Amazing." I nod before casually glancing in the direction of the stairs.

Sean takes a step toward me and looks into my eyes.

"I've been thinking about you all weekend," he says. "I wanted to call you, but I didn't know if your mom would answer....I can't believe we just ran into each other like this."

Another nervous glance at the stairs.

"I know," I say. "It's crazy."

"Want to get coffee or something?"

Another glance, and this time, he notices.

"Are you here with someone? Is it your mom?"

"No," I say. "I mean, yes, I'm here with someone. No, it's not my—"

"Hey, Kelly," Dave says as he walks up from the opposite direction. I see signs for an elevator over his head; of course he would come down that way. Dave stops right next to me, a little too close.

"What's up, Chancellor," Sean says. "Popular place."

96

"Guess so." Dave looks at me. "Are you ready to go?"

Even though I only glance at Sean, I see it: unfiltered jealousy. His eyes have clouded over; his dark eyebrows are knitted together like he's ready to take down the villain on his superhero planet. Except it's possible that right now the villain is me.

"You two came here together?" he asks, just to be sure. He looks at my dress accusingly.

"Yep," Dave says, stepping closer to me as if to mark his territory. I want to shove him away, but I think better of it. Mom's letting us date. It's a step in the right direction. If I mess this up, she'll never let us do it again.

And besides, Ella would kill me.

"I'm ready," I say. Dave turns to lead me out of the store. I put back the CD, and take a step away from Sean. "See you in class," I say quietly. There's nothing else to say.

Apparently, Sean agrees; he turns and walks away.

eleven

"Tell me about it again," Ella says at breakfast Monday morning. I wish she'd be more sensitive: She knows that the date ended with Dave and me running into Sean. The thought makes me sick.

"El, I told you everything yesterday when I got home," I say, rolling my eyes. "Twice." I'm still in pajamas; Mom was out running errands when I got up.

"You might've forgotten something," she says. "Let's just go over it again. I'm going to see him in less than an hour!"

Though I'm sure she knows the date backward and forward already, right down to little facts like the way he watched the entire movie with just his left foot up on the armrest in front of him, but not his right, I tell her again between bites of cereal, swallowing hard every time Sean enters my mind. Betsey must know what I'm thinking, because she chimes in when I pause too long—she's already memorized the details, too.

"But he didn't try to kiss you?" Ella asks when I'm finished. "Just the hug?" She looks a little defensive. Jealous. And why wouldn't she be? Someone who looks just like her stole her movie date.

"Just the hug," I reassure her.

"Show me how he did it," Ella says, standing from the table. She moves tentatively like she's not sure her twisted ankle is going to support her: It does. I look at her with my mouth open.

"You want me to do a hug reenactment?" I ask, laughing a little. She nods, smiling like a crazy person. I have that exact smile in my arsenal; I rarely use it, but when I glance at Betsey, I see that she's mirroring Ella's face exactly. It's a little creepy. "I'm totally not hugging you," I say, laughing again. "Not like *that*."

"Do it," Ella says. "Come on!"

"Ella!" I say. "You know what a hug feels like. It was just a hug." It's impossible not to think of Sean's arms around me on Friday night. *That* was a hug.

"Fine," she says, tsking and looking at me with a stern expression as she grabs her plate and takes it to the sink. Despite her hesitation a second ago, she's walking normally; Mom cleared her to go to school. "I guess I'll just have to try to get him to hug me again."

"I'm sure that won't be a problem for you," Betsey says, her mouth full.

"Definitely not," Ella says dreamily.

I glance at the clock, wondering when Mom will be back.

"Hey, you guys?" I say. "I need to talk to you about something." I'm thinking about it so much that I actually *dreamed* about Mom's secret office last night; I know I need to tell them about it. I wanted to do it sooner, but Mom had a very rare day off yesterday and she was home from the time I got back from the movies with Dave until we went to sleep last night. Maybe she even slept all night in her own bed for once. This is my first chance to talk to Ella and Betsey alone.

"Is everything all right?" Bet asks, looking at me curiously.

"Yes, but—"

"If everything's okay, can we talk tonight?" Ella interrupts. "I need to finish getting ready."

I open my mouth to explain that we should probably talk now—because I'm not sure where Mom will be later—but the buzzer beeps, telling us that the gate's opening. Mom's home.

"That's fine," I say. Then, not wanting to worry them, I add, "Really, it's no big deal. Tonight's great."

"It's a plan," Ella says before waving and leaving the kitchen. She heads up the stairs a little slower than usual because of her ankle, humming all the way. I've heard the song before: It's the one Dave played for me on the way to the movies.

At school I push thoughts of Mom out of my head and focus on Sean. The second I walk into creative writing, I can tell that he's still mad about seeing me with Dave at the mall. His posture is stiff and he's facing full front. It's probably my imagination, but it seems like he may have scooted his desk up an inch or two.

"Great," I mutter to myself as I walk up the row to my seat. I ease into my chair and take a deep breath. Rationally, it's probably okay that he's mad: I can't date him anyway. But emotionally, I can't take it. I know that I have to try to fix things with him or I'm going to have a breakdown of soap opera proportions.

"Sean," I whisper to his back. He ignores me.

"Sean," I whisper again. I reach forward and touch the back of his right arm. He doesn't flinch; he doesn't turn around.

"Sean!" I whisper louder. "I need to talk to you."

Finally, slowly, he turns halfway in his seat, not all the way like when he's talked to me before. Like when he's given me his full attention.

"What's up?" he says, no intensity in his voice, like I'm anyone.

"I need to talk to you about yesterday," I whisper. "I want to explain."

"No need," he says, shrugging like he doesn't care. His

voice is louder than mine, and that lack of intimacy almost stings worse than his words. "I'm good."

"Really, Sean—" I begin, but Natasha cuts in.

"Hey, Sean," she says, glancing at me with a smirk. "Show me that app you were talking about earlier." *Earlier?* Jealousy rushes through me, and I realize that this is how Sean must've felt when he saw me with Dave.

He pulls out his phone and starts talking to Natasha about a photo app, taking a picture of her and then doing something on the screen. Instead of letting the anger take over, I try to redirect my energy toward getting him to talk to me. And that requires a softer touch.

"Can I see?"

Sean looks at me, and in his eyes I can tell that he's conflicted—both wanting to hate me and wanting to move forward like nothing happened. In the few seconds he considers his next move, Natasha flashes me a look that screams *Back off!* But I persist.

"You're totally app-sessed," I joke, smiling warmly at him. It's silly, but it does its job: His face softens and he turns his body so both Natasha and I can see the screen. Class is going to start any moment; I only hope that before it does, I can melt the iceberg enough to get him to talk to me for real later.

"Anyway, this app's awesome," Sean says, looking at the screen, then Natasha, then glancing at me. "It's called Twinner. You know, like Twitter but with twins?"

"Got it," I say.

"Cool," Natasha says, a little too flirtatiously.

Sean goes on with the explanation. "You upload a photo of yourself and it uses facial recognition software to find your twin from all the photos on the Internet," he says as he holds the phone out so we can see it a little better. "See? We just found Natasha's."

On the screen, there's a picture of a girl with similar facial features but completely different hair and body type.

"She does look like you," I say to Natasha.

"She wishes," Natasha says, arching her back a little. Trying to control the look on my face, I think of my mirror images, Betsey and Ella. I can't help but wonder why anyone would want to feel less individual. Then I think that this app is Mom's worst nightmare.

Mom.

I think about how Mom's the reason I don't have my own, full identity in the first place. She's the reason I can't go out with Sean, the reason he's hurt and mad at me right now. She's hiding something from us—and I'm starting to feel like it's bigger than just a personal office space. It seems like my mom's more concerned with keeping herself out of trouble than she is with us.

Something has to change. It just has to.

"Do me," I say to Sean, driven by a fast and furious wave of rebellion.

"You wish," Natasha mutters under her breath before turning toward her friend in the other row, bored with the conversation since I joined. I blush a little, but Sean just ignores her; instead he starts typing on the keyboard.

"Don't you need a picture?" I ask.

"I have one," he says quietly, eyes on his phone. Relief floods through me.

"Here," he says after a few seconds. "That's actually the best match I've seen yet."

I'm not sure what I was expecting, but it wasn't this. When I take the phone from his outstretched hand, I gasp at the picture on the screen. The girl really looks like me. Like us. For a second I think it's actually Betsey or Ella, but then I realize that she looks a little older, and her face is rounder. But we all have the same eye and hair color, and the same curls.

"That's unbelievable," I say, handing Sean back the phone just before Mr. Ames tells him to put it away. There's a heavy feeling creeping through my stomach; a crazy thought trying to overtake my brain.

Is she the Original? Is she Beth?

"I can message her if you want," Sean says, glancing back at me.

"Huh?" I ask, distracted.

"Twinner doesn't give out names, but you can message people, and if they want to meet you, they can write back."

"Oh," I say, taking out my notebook and feeling like

my head's on two planets. He probably thinks I'm mental. Pulling it together, I say, "That's okay. It's a little creepy."

"If you say so."

Mr. Ames finishes writing on the board and moves to the podium.

"Sean?" I whisper.

"Yeah?"

"I still want to explain," I say. "About yesterday. It's not what you think."

There's a long pause; I think he might not answer. But then he does.

"I'll listen."

The day turns out all right. Sean assures me when the bell rings that his after-school plans are legitimate—he's going to take pictures with his mom—and not some excuse to get out of talking to me. After we say goodbye to each other at the end of the English hall, I walk to my locker feeling lighter than I did earlier. No one gets kicked in the head at cheer practice. And, when I get home, Mom's on her way out for work, so I don't have to deal with talking to her.

The hours pass, and eventually Betsey returns home.

"So, what's this about?" Bet asks when we're settled on couches. "Did you discover the meaning of life?"

"Funny," I say, not laughing. "No, this is sort of serious."

Ella and Betsey both give me their full attention. I'm

not sure of the best way to tell them the things I'm thinking. I start with the office space.

"The day Mom and I got in that fight, remember I followed her?" I ask. Both of them nod in unison, synchronized like they're doing it on purpose.

"How could we forget that day?" Ella asks. Her tone is joking, but it stings nonetheless. Betsey smacks her on the arm.

"Anyway," I say, "Mom said she was running errands, but she wasn't."

"What'd she do?" Ella asks, face scrunched up in confusion.

"She went to a small office building," I say. Bet's face scrunches up, too. "I thought maybe she had an appointment or something, but then she got out and unlocked the door. With her own key. Like the office is hers."

"What?" Bet asks. "Why?"

"I have no idea," I say. "But it's weird, don't you think?"

"Are you sure you don't just think you saw her unlock it?" Ella asks. "Maybe—"

"She unlocked it."

"That's so strange," Ella says. "I mean, she already has an office here, and probably one at the hospital, too."

"Why would she need another one?" Betsey asks, finishing Ella's thought.

We're all quiet; there are only so many times I can say

"I don't know." I let it sink in before bringing up the second thing. I tell them about the Twinner app, and about how I let Sean use a photo of me to find my twin.

"Lizzie!" Ella shouts. "That was really stupid!"

"Maybe," I say, "or maybe not. But that's not the point. The point is that a match came back. She looks like us; older, but otherwise just like us."

I listen to the clock tick; we stare at one another. Finally, Betsey speaks.

"You think it's her, don't you?" she asks excitedly. Betsey's always been the one most fascinated by the girl we call Beth. "You think she's the Original."

"Probably not," I say. I hesitate. "But what if she is?"

"Impossible," Ella says. "That would mean that Mom lied, which doesn't make sense. Why would she tell us so much about how we were created but lie about the fact that the Original was dead?"

"Maybe she didn't want us to be able to find her," Betsey offers. Her dark eyes are sparkling like she's been given a mission. "Maybe there's something about her Mom doesn't want us to know."

"Maybe you're bonkers," Ella says, reaching over to grab a handful of tortilla chips.

"Well, maybe Mom doesn't know, either," I say. "Maybe the clients lied to the researchers about the Original being dead. Maybe they just wanted a spare for—"

"Ew," Betsey says, "a spare kid? Like a spare tire?"

"There are messed-up people in the world," I say, shrugging. "You never know. But honestly, my money's on Mom being the one who lied to us."

"You're just pissed at her about Sean," Betsey says. "You don't really think that."

"Don't I?" I ask sarcastically. "She's hiding an office from us; what else is she hiding? It's entirely plausible that she lied about the Original, too. That the baby didn't die and for some reason, she doesn't want us to know." I pause, and a thought hits me. "For all we know, she could be hiding Beth in that weird secret office of hers."

"Come on," Betsey says, rolling her eyes. "This is Mom we're talking about."

"If you're so convinced, follow her again," Ella says between crunches, like stalking our mother is the most normal thing on earth. I look at her funny. "Seriously. I mean, you're probably wrong—it's probably something totally innocent. Maybe she was taking care of a colleague's office while they were traveling or something. Just follow her again and you'll know for sure."

In the middle of the night, when I'm still awake envisioning talk show–style reunions with our long-lost DNA donor, when I'm still conjuring up images of what could be happening at Mom's secret office, I pull on a sweatshirt and tiptoe out of my room and into the hall. I listen at doorways to see if anyone else is awake; when all I hear is nothing, I move quietly down the stairs. For a moment, I consider acting on Ella's advice: driving back to Mom's office and trying harder to get in. But the horror movie–style scary factor of that gives me the chills inside my warm house. I opt to poke around Mom's office at home instead.

Nothing's different from the last time I visited—even the emergency money stash is still forty dollars low. I pull open the bottom drawer and see the stacks of correspondence from Wyoming. The same feeling of curiosity overtakes me that I had the last time I was here. I take out one of the stacks and remove a bank statement from its neatly ripped-open envelope.

Back before we moved, Mom talked on the phone a lot to a guy we jokingly call the Wizard. She won't tell us anything about him, just that he's a friend and he helps her sometimes. One such time was when he advised her to filter money through a corporation in another state; hers is called Trifecta, Inc., and it's based in Wyoming. We have a double layer of protection—the fake corporation and new identities. Two new identities, of course: one for her and one for the three of us.

Mom said she was paid well for the cloning, which is why she's been able to provide for us. But she's always maintained that she needed an outside job, too. However, as I look at the bank statement from the last month, something strange catches my eye: Twenty thousand dollars was deposited on the first of the month.

I open another statement and my jaw drops: Another twenty thousand dollars was deposited on the first of that month, too. I find another statement and another twenty grand. There must be more than twenty statements, all revealing deposits in the same amount.

Excitedly, feeling like I've caught Mom at something, I put everything back and run upstairs. I turn on my computer and do an Internet search for ER doctors' average salary. When the results pop up, I'm disappointed. They can make around $250,000 a year: Even math-challenged me knows that's more than twenty thousand a month.

I laugh a little at myself for getting worked up over nothing before turning off the computer and climbing back into bed. Even though the fact remains that I saw Mom unlock that office, maybe Ella's right that it's something completely benign. Maybe she really is watering someone else's plants.

Feeling silly, I push thoughts of Mom from my head and think of Sean until I fall asleep.

twelve

Creative writing is a work period and in the middle of class, Sean asks if I want to hang out after practice. He says it so easily, reminding me that hanging out after school is what most kids do. Most kids don't rush home so the evening clone can leave the house.

"I...can't," I say. Sean looks at me hard, like he can't figure me out.

"Okay," he says before refocusing on his writing project. "I thought you wanted to talk."

There's a shift in the air between us. I want to say something, to explain. I want to tell him that I'd like nothing better than to spend the afternoon with him. But I can't, so I look down at my own work.

"I'm not really into games," he says quietly. I look up to see that he's still facing front, but his chin is a little to the right so I can hear him.

"I'm not playing games," I whisper.

"It seems like you are," he says, less angry and more stoic. He sighs. "I don't get you, Lizzie."

It feels awful, but what am I going to do about it in the middle of writing class? In the middle of my third of a life? So far, from his perspective, I've alternated between flirting with him—even telling him to kiss me—and being seen with David...or not at all. I can see how he'd think I'm playing games.

"I'm sorry," I murmur, meaning it.

Sean doesn't talk to me for the rest of the period, and when class is over, he says "See ya" with no feeling, confusion written all over his face.

I'm completely distracted at cheer. Morgan slams into me at one point, because she moves when she's supposed to, but like I'm stuck in the mud, I do not.

"That's your spot," Morgan says, pointing at the ground a few steps to the right. "This is mine," she says, pointing at where I'm standing. She blows her bangs out of her eyes, frustrated, and rubs her shoulder.

"Sorry," I say. "I'm having a day."

"Whatever," she says in a way that feels about something more than the collision. She walks away, and I swear I hear her talking about me to a few of the other girls. I manage to hit my mark the next few times, but then at the end of practice the day devolves even more when a bunch of the girls decide to get pizza and invite me to go.

"My mom asked me to come straight home today," I say. "Next time?"

"Sure," Isla says, smiling. "Next time."

I know that there won't be any "next time" until I get my life back—and that getting my life back isn't a priority for Mom. Between that and being weighed down by the frustration of things with Sean, I drive through a haze of tears the whole way home.

Mom's car is gone and the main floor of the house is deserted when I arrive. I grab a snack and head upstairs; no one's in the rec room. Ella's door's closed; when I knock, she doesn't answer, so I peek in. She's sitting cross-legged with books covering the entire top of her bed, bopping her head to music playing through earbuds. She doesn't see me, and she looks so content that I don't want to bring her down with my drama. I back out and close the door behind me.

I glance into my bedroom, then Mom's, in search of Bet. She's nowhere to be found. I go back downstairs and walk through the kitchen and the living room, and finally end up in the office. At first, I don't think she's there, but then I see feet peeking out from behind the desk. I walk around and find Betsey with papers all over her lap.

Bet screams when she sees me, which startles me and catapults both of us into hysterical laughter.

"What are you *doing?*" I ask when I can breathe enough to talk.

"Snooping, obviously," she says. "I thought you were Mom!"

"Hardly," I say, scoffing. "Snooping for what?" I sit down next to her as she blushes and looks away. "Bet? What are you looking for?"

"Okay, fine," she says, "I admit that your little theory about the Original being alive piqued my interest. I mean, it *is* sort of weird that the girl on Twinner matched us exactly. I just thought maybe—if it *was* Mom who lied—maybe she kept something about Beth in the office."

"Probably not this one," I mutter. It's funny that Betsey's snooping today after I did the same thing last night.

"I guess that's a good point," Bet says, tossing her curly hair out of her face. Instinctively, I wipe away my own hair even though I don't need to: Sometimes the others' sensations are contagious like yawns. "Well, that was a pointless search. Guess I'd better put this stuff back."

"I'll help you," I say, grabbing a few stray papers and organizing them into a stack. Then I remember something about Twinner. "You know, Bet, Sean said that you can message the matches—maybe you should get an account and try it? I mean, you never know."

Betsey looks at me with excitement in her eyes. Maybe I'm reading too much into it, but it seems like she needs something to preoccupy her right now, like maybe she's as unsettled about our situation as I am.

"Maybe I will," she says. "Thanks, Lizzie."

I smile, happy to have done something to make her feel better. "Anytime."

I wake up at midnight, heart pounding, sweating, distressed after a nightmare about Sean marrying Natasha. Rationally, I know we're teenagers and no one's marrying anyone, but when in the dream he turned and looked at me from the altar and said, "This could've been you," it felt like the worst thing that's ever happened to me.

I take several deep breaths to try to calm myself, but when it doesn't work, I get up for water. I walk into the hallway, and Ella's opening her door, looking fearful.

"What happened?" she asks, seconds before Betsey opens hers.

"I just had a bad dream," I say to both of them. "Sorry if I woke you up."

"Are you okay?" Betsey asks, coming closer and touching my arm. "You look really pale."

"Maybe I'm getting sick or something." Truthfully, it's more likely that I'm lovesick.

"No, really, Lizzie, what's up?" Ella asks. The concern in her voice brings tears to my eyes.

"I'm just...I'm losing Sean," I say, which doesn't make sense, since I'm not allowed to date him in the first place.

But somehow it does to me. And they can feel my emotion: It makes sense to them, too.

"I'm so sorry," Betsey says, hugging me. "I wish I knew how to solve it."

Something I've been thinking about but haven't had the guts to bring up just falls out of my mouth now. "I want to tell him," I say into her shoulder. Betsey pulls back and looks at me, surprised.

"What are you talking about?" Ella asks, surprised, too, and a little snippy. "There's no way that you're saying you want to tell him about...us. *Right?*"

I wipe under my eyes and look from Ella to Betsey without saying anything.

"Wow," Betsey mutters as Ella's mouth drops.

"You can't be serious," Ella says. "Mom would have a fit of infinite proportions."

"If she found out," I say.

"We've never told anyone," Bet says. "At least I haven't." She looks at us funny. "Have you guys?"

"No!" Ella says definitively.

"No," I say. "I've never liked anyone enough to *want* to tell them." I look at Ella. "I mean, don't you sort of want to tell Dave? To let him know you for you?"

"I'd be lying if I said the thought hasn't crossed my mind," Ella says, folding her arms over her chest, "but I'd never do it. We made a pact."

"When we were *kids*," Betsey says, and I can tell she's on my side.

"Still," Ella says, "we could get Mom into serious trouble. And if she goes to jail, what happens to us? Mom's parents are dead—we have no family. Do we go into foster care? Or does the government take us into custody and examine us like lab rats for the rest of our lives? I just don't think it's worth it."

"You watch too much TV," I say, smiling a little to ease the tension. "And besides, those things would only be a concern if Sean told someone else. Which he wouldn't."

"You hardly know him," Ella says. "How do you know you can trust him? That *we* can trust him?"

"I just know." I can't help but smile because it's the truth. "I just have this feeling; I'm positive that he'll keep our secret." I pause, searching the faces that I know by heart because they're copies of my own. "I want to tell him, both for him and for me. I want to let him in."

We're all quiet for a few moments; the house creaks like it's joining the conversation. In the end, there are no more words spoken. But the look on Betsey's face, then the subtle nod from Ella, tell me that tonight at this haphazard meeting in the dark hallway, we three have made a major decision for ourselves for perhaps the first time in our lives. I know without words that they're okay with it.

We're telling Sean; we're letting someone else in.

And we're doing it whether Mom likes it or not.

thirteen

"What are you doing right now?" I ask, blocking Sean's path out of the classroom. My phone's in my hand, the email from Betsey still on the screen.

She left early. You're in the clear.

"Standing in the aisle," he says jokingly, but it comes out a little too sarcastic. I know he's still confused: He was stand-offish all period. I'm so nervous I think I might get sick.

I take a deep breath. "What I meant was: What are you doing after school?"

"Oh," he says. "Yeah, I figured." He pulls his backpack onto his shoulder and glances at the door: We're the only people left in the classroom. "I'm probably just going home. Why?"

"I wanted to ask you..." I say, confidence seeping out of me with every passing second. I had it all planned out earlier, before I was actually standing in front of him. "I...do you want to come to my house for a little while? I still want to talk to you, and I need to...show you something."

"At your house?" he asks, still confused, but curious, too. It calms me a bit.

"At my house." I nod once.

"Don't you have cheer?" he asks.

I force a cough. "I'm sick."

"Okay, sure," Sean says, smiling. "Lead the way."

"This is where you live?" Sean asks, squinting down into the forest fortress twenty minutes later. His car is parked out on the main road and he's next to me in the sedan just outside the gate. All you can see from up here is a small part of the roof.

"I don't like Dave," I say, ignoring his question.

Sean glances at me and says, "It's none of my business." I hope it's just a defense mechanism; the aloofness bothers me.

"Do you seriously feel that way?" I ask quietly, eyes on the gate. "Because if you do, then—"

"No," he interrupts. He looks away, out the window at nothing. "You're making me crazy."

"Good," I say, smiling. "I mean, not good, but good that you...care."

"I care."

"Okay."

I inhale deeply and blow it out. Then I punch the buttons to open the gate.

"So, as I was saying, I don't like Dave," I reiterate as I navigate the driveway with less fear than usual. "I mean, he's nice enough, but I don't like him in that way." Pause. *Say it.* "I like you."

I look at Sean and catch his half smile as he looks down at his hands. Then his eyes are on mine. "Then what's with hanging out with him?"

"That's one of the things I want to try to explain," I say, parking in front of the garage. I turn off the car; he looks at me, ready to listen. "Not here," I say. "Not in the car, I mean. We have to go inside. But I'm just warning you, I'm going to tell you some strange stuff. Your normal day ends now."

Sean smiles at me like he did that night at the game. "I think I can handle it."

I pause on the porch, thinking of all that's about to change. Wondering for a beat if I'm doing the right thing, then remembering how confidently I told Ella and Betsey that we can trust Sean. Because we can; I know we can. And I wasn't kidding when I said that I needed to tell him for me, too. I need to get my life back, a step at a time. Step one: Grab the door handle. I push through, my heart thumping hard in my chest.

"Come in," I say quietly.

He walks tentatively into the house and immediately

looks up. It's hard not to do: The soaring ceiling with the colossal crystal chandelier in the center is attention grabbing, to say the least. Sean's eyes travel up the grand staircase and across the balcony until they meet walls where the bedrooms are. I watch as they continue to meander up, up, and up.

I clear my throat.

"Sorry," he says, eyes on me now. "But your house is sweet."

"Thanks," I say, kicking off my shoes. Sean copies me, and I start up the stairs. "Let's go."

I pause on the second step from the top. I know that they know we're coming—their nervousness is making mine snowball. I turn to face Sean; he's two steps behind me, so I'm taller than him. "Ready?" I ask.

"Okay, now you're starting to freak me out." My face must look as worried as I feel, because he grabs my hand. "Hey," he whispers, "I'm fine."

I nod, then turn and finish the climb, still holding his hand. The double doors to the rec room are open; Ella and Betsey are sitting on opposite couches. They both turn to look at us.

"Hi, you two," Betsey says warmly. Ella waves stiffly.

"Hi," I say back before glancing at Sean. His eyes float from face to face. As planned, we're all in different clothes, but still, I'm sure it's a lot to take in.

"Are you guys triplets or something?" he asks, following me into the rec room after I tug a little on his hand.

121

Ella laughs and it's higher pitched than usual. Sean and I sit down in the open chairs.

"No," I say, "at least not anymore." Sean looks at me funny; I gesture to the others. "That's Betsey, and this is Ella." They both smile at him, and I wonder if it seems like he's looking at two copies of me. It makes me feel the opposite of special.

Average.

But I force myself to get over it and do what I brought him here to do. "Sean, there's no easy way to say this, so I'll just go for it," I say, sitting up a little straighter. He looks at me again.

"The thing is that we're not triplets," I say. "We wish we were triplets. We used to think that we were, back when we were little. But really, what we are is...well, we're clones."

Part of me wonders whether Sean's going to stand and run out of the room screaming, but he doesn't move at first. His eyes stay on mine; his expression is expectant, like I'm going to shout, "Just kidding!" and we're all going to have a big laugh. But then, about five seconds later, his features give it away when he realizes I'm serious. The upturned corners of his lips flatten out, his eyebrows dip just slightly enough to make him look disbelieving. I could swear his grip on my hand loosens. I loosen mine, too, and our hands fall apart, into the space between our chairs. That space feels like a valley; I knit my hands together in my lap.

"What does that even mean?" Sean asks, looking at the others. Betsey scoots forward to the edge of her chair.

"It means that scientists created us in a lab from someone else's DNA," she says, sounding like a mixture of teacher and mother. "We were implanted into our mom's womb and came into the world just like you did."

I've never been so aware of how much Betsey's voice matches mine as I am in this second. I hate that Sean's probably aware of it, too.

"You look exactly alike," he says, eyeing us. I'm increasingly anxious until he looks at me and says quietly, "Almost." It makes my stomach flutter and it calms me. A little.

"We do look alike," Betsey says, "but maybe less alike than identical twins. We're copies of someone else, while twins start out as the same person but the egg splits apart into two people."

"How's that different?" Sean asks.

"A copy's never as good as the original," Ella jumps in. "Our Original might have been smarter than us. Or taller. And we probably have other differences because we were grown in our mom's eggs and not her mom's eggs."

Sean's eyes widen a little. "Is this why you were freaked out by Twinner?" he asks me. "You don't think that girl is the one—"

Ella and Betsey talk at the same time.

"Maybe," Bet says.

"No," Ella says.

I just shrug. "Our mom told us that the baby died."

"How did this even happen?" Sean asks.

I sigh; this is not going how I planned. But I'm determined to share this side of myself with Sean, so I begin to explain.

"Before we came along, our mom was a well-known scientist at a federally funded genetics lab. Of course, the government didn't know this, but the lab was working on human cloning in private. One day, this rich couple approached the head of the lab, Mom's boss, Dr. Jovovich, and secretly offered him and his team a boatload of money to basically bring back their baby daughter who died."

"Are you serious?" Sean says, looking horrified. "That's like a movie."

"Completely," I say, answering both questions with one word. When he doesn't ask anything else, I go on.

"Anyway, the scientists agreed, and after tests, they determined that the problem might have been a genetic disorder from the mother, so they decided that they'd need to implant the DNA into a different host's eggs before they were put in the client's womb. Mom volunteered her eggs, as she was the only woman on the project. The clients were presented with a full medical history on the egg donor, but never knew it was our mom.

"Around the time when the DNA was implanted into the eggs but before they were put into the mother, the father shared that he and his wife wanted only one of the three viable eggs—the best one—and they wanted to destroy the rest. Mom thought they wanted to make sure that the scientists wouldn't secretly grow the others in the name of research.

"Mom was probably way too involved in the project at this point, and because she was the egg donor, she sort of felt a claim to us. She didn't want any of us being discarded. So she and her boss came up with a plan: He'd put the eggs in Mom's womb instead and she'd disappear, and then he'd tell the clients that there had been an accident in the lab and all the eggs were destroyed."

"Your mom stole you and raised you herself," Sean says, looking a little pale. I nod. "But you weren't hers," he says quietly.

"We didn't come from her DNA, so no, not technically," Betsey says, "but she used her own eggs, and she gave birth to us. She raised us. We're hers."

"Oh," Sean says like he's not really buying it. Like he thinks Mom did something wrong. I try to make him see that what she did was *good*. Because as much as I hate living as a third of a person, I'm living at all because of her.

"She did it to protect us," I say. "We moved and lived as triplets, and we had a happy childhood."

"Then why don't you live as triplets now?" he asks.

I tell him the story of when we were nine and Dr. Jovovich was publicly arrested. "He admitted on the stand during his trial that there could be a set of three female clones our age living somewhere in the United States. Girl triplets went under the microscope and Mom freaked out. We went into hiding."

Sean stares at me; I clarify.

"We each do a third of the day."

"What do you mean?" he asks.

"I mean Ella goes to school until lunch, I do the afternoon classes and cheer practice, and Betsey does our night job and college class, and any other evening activities."

"But the ones who aren't at school are homeschooled in the same classes," Ella adds, like she doesn't want him to think we each only have a third of a brain, too.

"You're telling me that since you were ten years old, you've only been allowed out of the house one-third of each day?" he asks me, incredulous.

"Nine," I say, "but yeah."

"It's not really that we aren't *allowed* out," Ella says. "It's just our system."

Sean turns his body to face mine and there's an intensity in his eyes that I haven't seen before. "This is what you meant when you said your mom is strict?" he asks quietly, but doesn't wait for me to answer. "I mean, this is more than strict. This is...Lizzie, do you realize how messed up it is?"

I'm quiet a few seconds; it's possible that the others are holding their breath. Then, "I think you get used to things," I say. "I think you just go with your reality." I sigh before adding, "But I know how strange it must seem to you."

I'm about to tell him that it's strange to me now, too, when he runs his hands through his hair and stands up.

"I'm going to go get some air, okay?"

"Okay," I say, unsure whether that means he's going to open a window or flee the scene. But when he jogs down the stairs and goes out the front door, I get my answer.

"That went well," Ella mutters after he's gone.

"Shh," Betsey snaps at her. She nods in my direction, knowing I'm on edge. Probably feeling it. "He'll be back."

At first, I think Betsey's right. But then a half hour passes, and someone turns on the TV for background noise. The cell phone buzzes and my heart leaps out of my chest; I can't hide my disappointment when I discover that it's just one of the cheerleaders checking to see why I'm not at practice.

"I should skip work, in case one of them happens to go to the restaurant after practice," Betsey says.

"If you want to," I mutter before glancing at the clock for what must be the hundredth time.

Bet leaves to call in sick, and Ella drapes a blanket over her lap and turns up the volume. She's really watching now: It's not just background anymore.

My insides rage with nervousness: I *need* Sean to call me.

Two hours after he leaves, the others force me into the kitchen for sustenance. We opt for a cocktail party–style dinner: crackers with cream cheese and jalapeño peppers, microwaved chicken skewers, carrot sticks with ranch, and cut-up fruit. My eyes are tearing up from putting too many jalapeño slices on my last cracker when there's a knock on the door so faint that I barely hear it.

"What was that?" I ask.

"The door?" Bet says.

"I'll get it," Ella offers. But I shove her aside and run down the hall and across the entryway. Just before I open the door, I realize that Sean's shoes are still here, where he kicked them off.

"Where have you been?" I ask when we're face-to-face.

"Out here," he says. "Getting some air."

"For two hours?" I ask. "I thought you left."

"No," he says, "I just needed to think. You weren't kidding when you said the normal part of my day was over. I think the normal part of my life is over."

"Want to come back in?" I ask. "Or are you just here for your shoes?"

"Actually, I'm here for you," he says quietly. "But I'll take my shoes, too."

I inhale salty air and gently brush my hair out of my mouth as Sean and I drive, windows down, away from my house. It's a warm day, but it's nearly October so there's a little bite to it; I'd like to roll up the windows, but I guess Sean's need for air continues. I keep looking at him, trying to mentally yank his thoughts out of his brain with the help of my eyeballs.

"I have a million questions," he says finally. I exhale, relieved.

"I have a million answers," I say. "Go for it."

"Okay," he says, turning a corner and turning down the radio. Then, noticing me shiver, he apologizes and rolls up the windows. "Was Ella in creative writing this year? At first?" He glances at me and I smile.

"Good eye," I say. "I failed a trig quiz and Mom made us switch. My first day was the day I fainted."

"I thought so," he says. "You were so much cooler after that day." He pauses, then adds, "I mean, not that Ella's not cool."

"No, it's okay," I say. "I get it. Thank you."

"Sure," he says. "So my next question is: Why didn't your mom just move to another country when you were babies? Why'd she stay in the U.S.?"

"She's not some international spy or something," I say, laughing. "She probably just wanted to stay in the country she knew. I think she really thought hiding us in plain sight would work."

"I see," he says, pulling onto the freeway. He thinks for a second. "Okay, what about your system: Why do you split each day in thirds instead of just doing every third day?"

"We tried that once; it didn't work," I say. "It was too hard to keep up on classes if we were only in them every third day. And South had block scheduling, so that made it really hard. This works better."

Sean pauses before firing off another question. "So, what's it like?" he asks finally. "Looking exactly like two other people?"

The question is one I've never been asked, not even when I was young. It's complicated.

"Well, it's equal parts wonderful and horrible," I say.

"What's good about it?"

"The connection." I smile. "We're really close, and not just emotionally. We're on one another's wavelengths. We can feel strong feelings from the other ones, and sometimes we even have the same dreams."

"That's so cool," he says. I nod.

"Sometimes, yes," I say. "Like if I'm in a bad mood, they just know. They can feel what I feel. They don't have to ask. It's nice to be understood like that."

"What about the bad parts?" Sean asks as he takes a hard turn. I realize that we're near the water now.

"I think it's made worse by the fact that we're sharing one life, but the bad side of looking like two other people is feeling like I don't have my own identity at all. Like there's nothing unique about me."

I pause, remembering what Sean said earlier.

"I agree with you, you know," I say. "About how my life is messed up."

"I figured," he says as he pulls into a beach lot. He parks the car and turns off the ignition. He turns to me and grabs my hand. "Listen, Lizzie, I'm not going to pretend that I'm not completely floored by what you told me this afternoon. I'm going to have a lot more questions—and I gotta be honest: I don't know her, but I think your mom is off the rails."

"That's okay. You might be right."

"But I'm glad you told me," he says quietly. "I'm glad that you're not just trying to date me and Dave at the same time."

I roll my eyes at him. "Ella's dating Dave," I say. "I hope I'm dating you."

"I hope I'm dating you, too."

Sean and I get out, he grabs a bag from the trunk, and we hold hands as we walk across Big Beach. Mid-fall and probably snowing in other parts of the country; here it's a beautiful late afternoon and a few families and groups of friends are out. There's even a small circle of wet-suit-clad surfers on the water despite the fact that the waves are surely growing colder.

Our secret out, I'm not weightless like I'd like to be, but I'm not quite as burdened, either. "You know, you're the only person we've ever told," I say to him.

He looks at me, surprised. "Seriously?"

"Seriously. There's never been anyone we were close to, except a neighbor in Florida. But we were triplets then . . . so there was nothing to tell."

"I'm sorry you haven't had anyone to share stuff with," he says, squeezing my hand. "But at the same time, I'm sort of honored to be the first." He smiles a silly smile. "It's like I'm the chosen one."

"You're the chosen dork," I say, shaking my head. I realize we're walking toward a wall of rocks; I hope he doesn't think I'm climbing over it.

"Hey, Lizzie?" I look at his face. "Jokes aside, I'm glad you told me. As much as I might need time to process, I'm glad I know. I'm glad you trust me enough to let me in."

"I'm glad, too," I say just as we stop in front of the rocks. I furrow my brow at him.

"Now I need you to trust me again."

"Oh, really?" I ask, playfulness in my tone. It feels nice. He points to an opening between two massive boulders.

"You want me to go in there?"

He nods. "It's amazing; you'll see."

"What if there are wild animals hiding in the darkness?"

"There aren't," he says, grinning.

"Are you sure?" I take a step closer and try to peer inside, but all I can see is blackness.

"I'm sure. It's just a passage. My dad used to bring me here all the time when I was a kid, back before my parents split. I come back sometimes to veg out or take pictures or whatever."

"Or *whatever*," I tease, a touch jealous. "Been here a lot, have you?" I take another step closer to the rocks.

"I've never brought another girl here, if that's what you mean."

Sean laughs, but it reassures me just the same; when he leads me into what looks like a cave, I feel reasonably safe. Then when we wind through and pop out the other side, I feel like I've just won the emotional lottery. The cove before me is a three-walled room with an open window to the ocean: the most beautiful escape I could ever imagine.

"It's our own personal beach," I murmur, looking out toward the water.

"Mm-hmm," Sean says, taking out his camera and setting the bag in the sand. Out of the corner of my eye, I see him focusing on my profile. He's standing next to and a little behind me, so I know that the background of the photo is water crashing on the far wall of rocks. I don't hear the shutter snap, because the waves are too loud, but I hear what Sean says next.

"I'm glad to know you aren't crazy." I flip in his direction; he's smirking at me.

"What are you talking about?"

He shrugs, snaps another photo of my now-surprised-slash-irritated expression, then answers. "I thought you might've had split personalities or something," he says. "Because Ella and you are so . . ."

"Different," I say. We quietly take each other in for a few seconds.

"You were wrong earlier," he says.

"Oh, yeah? About what?"

"About not being unique. I mean, I know you look like Ella and Betsey. But I don't see the three of you the same way. You're . . . you."

The waves crash; I shiver in the ocean breeze. Neither of us speaks for a few more moments.

"Can I take some pictures of you?" Sean asks sweetly. I smile and nod, happy to be moving on from the day's heavy discussion to do something light.

We spend the next two hours snapping shot after shot. I climb onto a low rock and he takes a series of pictures of me standing there like a warrior. I sit on a log, legs outstretched, and Sean snaps a few close-ups of my face. I take off my shoes and consider wading into the water until I realize it's too chilly. He takes a few photos of my toes before I put my shoes back on. I drop into the sand and laugh as Sean click, click, clicks from every angle, eventually having to use a flash when the fall day grows dark.

I feel silly at first, but Sean's encouraging words put me at ease. I've never had an interest in modeling—or the size-zero frame that goes with it—but with Sean peering out from behind the camera, it feels much more intimate than just taking pretty pictures.

It feels more like making out.

I roll to my side in the sand, head propped on my hand. Sean's on his stomach next to me, camera pointed at my face.

"Are you glad you came over today?" I ask softly. The waves crash.

"More than glad," Sean says from behind the camera. "Thankful." Click.

"Truly?" I ask. "Because you did hide for two hours."

"I just needed to think about everything," he says. "To let it sink in."

"Yeah," I say. "I'll probably do that when I try to go to sleep tonight. It was a pretty big deal for me."

"I know it was," he says. "Are you glad you did it?"

"Yes," I say without hesitation.

"Good," he says, putting the camera back up to his face. "I do have one question, though."

My heart skips; it's the tone of his voice.

Click.

"You said Betsey does evening stuff," he says.

"Yes," I answer, half smiling.

Click.

"Football games are in the evening."

"Oh, really?" I feign surprise.

Click.

"There's one game in particular I'm curious about," Sean says, still from behind the camera.

"It was me," I whisper just before the waves crash.

Sean lowers the camera and pulls the lens cap out of his pocket. He snaps it on and sets the camera aside. Then he scoots over to me. With his face two inches from mine, he whispers:

"Prove it."

And I do.

fourteen

The next day after school, I'm driving down the road when Mom's driving up. When we pass each other, I see that she's wearing her scrubs, so she must be going to work. I get a flash of nervous excitement, wondering if I should take the opportunity to check out her secret office during the day. I make a split decision to do it; I pull over and turn around.

Mom's so far ahead of me I can't see her, but then half-way down the hill, I notice her turning in the opposite direction of work.

"Here we go again," I mutter to myself. "Where are you going this time?"

I follow, realizing after a few minutes that we're tracing the path back to the office.

"You're going to be late for work!" I say aloud, annoyed at her. The cell rings; it's Home.

"You're late," Betsey says.

"I know, sorry," I say. "I'm following Mom."

"Really?" Bet asks, her voice going up a little. "To the hospital?"

"No, I saw her leaving and was going to take the chance when she's at work to check out that office, but she's driving there instead. In fact, wait, hold on a sec." I put down the phone so I can use two hands to pull into a space. "Okay, I'm back. I had to park. She's going in now."

I watch and tell Betsey as Mom pulls keys from her purse and unlocks the door. She goes in, and I wait.

"What's happening now?" Bet asks five minutes later, after growing tired of hearing about how cute Sean was in class today.

"Still nothing," I say.

"What, she's just hanging out in there?"

"I guess," I say, sighing.

"Well, come back," she says. "I'm going to be late for class."

"Fine," I say, shaking my head. We hang up, and I'm about to turn the key in the ignition when I decide to go try to look inside. If Mom catches me, she'll be mad, but no madder than she is already.

I hop out and jog across the street, then hug the side of the building. When I'm in front, I get such a surge of nervousness that I consider turning back, but something keeps me going forward. I walk in my mom's footsteps up the stairs and cup my hands so I can peer in the window next to the front door. Part of me thinks she's going to be standing there, staring out. Thankfully, she's not.

Inside is just an ordinary doctor's or dentist's office with a reception desk in front—except that there's no receptionist, and there are no waiting area chairs or decorations, either. The front room is empty. I look for a few minutes, then decide to leave, but just before I pull away, I see Mom pass by the doorway to the back area. She's reading something, moving from the left side of the building to the right side, engrossed. She has a pen in her mouth, and she looks like she's . . . working? Except that she's not at the hospital. And she's no longer wearing her scrubs.

Confused, I back away and jog to the car, looking over my shoulder every so often to make sure Mom's not watching me. Distractedly, I make one stop before I go home. Then I drive back to the house even faster. When I arrive, I burst through the front door and call for Betsey and Ella. Ella appears from the direction of the kitchen; Betsey looks down at me curiously from the balcony.

"Mom's not an ER doctor," I say, out of breath for seemingly no reason. "Someone's paying her twenty thousand dollars every month and it's sure as hell not Memorial Hospital."

The others are speechless for a few moments. Then finally, Ella speaks.

"Huh," she says, looking stupefied. "I guess I was wrong about the watering-plants thing, then?"

"Yeah," I say, running a hand through my hair. "I guess you were."

fifteen

At noon on Saturday, we three are scattered around the rec room talking in circles. Mom said she was working a double shift—which means she's probably at her secret office—but wherever she is, I'm glad that the house and the day are ours.

"So, are we going to confront her about it?" Ella asks, looking uneasy about her own question. She went along with the whole Sean thing, but I think that in general, deep down, she's afraid of change. Plus she's dating Dave, so her life has actually improved lately.

"She'll probably just lie," Betsey says, putting her feet up on the coffee table. "I mean, she's lied to us for years about her job—"

"And about where her money comes from," I interject.

"Right," Bet says, "so what's to stop her from just lying her way out of this?" She pauses. "I wish that girl from Twinner would get back to me. I mean, what if it's really Beth? If we had that to throw at Mom—if we could catch her in *that* lie—then she'd be forced to tell us the rest."

"I think the Twinner thing's a coincidence," Ella says. "I think she's just a girl who happens to look sort of like us."

"*Exactly* like us," Betsey corrects her.

"In a picture," Ella says. "Maybe not in real life. Whatever. I think we need to focus on Mom and why she's lying, and what she's really doing all night when she says she's at work."

"And we're back to the question of confronting her or not," I say before sighing. We're all quiet for a minute, and I realize that the stereo's on: It's so low it sounds like it's coming from another house.

"I can't think when I'm starving," Betsey says finally. "Someone go get pizza."

"You're so lazy," I say, rolling my eyes.

"Let's get it from that place where Dave works," Ella says, her ulterior motives shining bright as a neon sign.

"It's afternoon," Betsey says to me, "which means you're the one who should go. I mean, I'd be happy to go, and I'm sure Ella would, too, but it's your time." She smiles at me devilishly, like she knows she's won.

"Why don't you go with me?" I ask, challenging her. "I mean, if you're so happy to go."

Betsey waits a beat, then says, "Okay."

"What?" Ella asks. "If anyone's going, I am. You guys don't even like Dave."

"Is he working today?" I ask. Ella shrugs.

"Well, I actually do want to go, because I need to pick up some new deodorant at the store next to the pizza place," I say. "You guys always get the wrong kind."

"Stan's is in that complex," Bet says. "Get ice cream, too."

"I thought you were going with me," I say, smirking.

"Oh, right, I am," Betsey says, and I can't tell if she's kidding.

"You're not seriously both going," Ella says.

Betsey and I hold gazes for a few seconds, and then, when soundless words have passed between us, we both look at Ella. "Let's all go," I say. Betsey nods, then stands up.

"We can't," Ella says, but I know she really wants to see if Dave's at the pizza place.

"Sure we can," Betsey says. She's already in the doorway. "Mom's out. And besides, if she catches us, we'll just ask her where she was today."

"But what if someone sees us?" Ella protests even as she's following me down the stairs.

"Ella, I'm not convinced there are any 'someones' who care about us anymore. And if there are, at this point, I might just take my chances."

"Go, Lizzie!" Betsey says happily, opening the front door.

And then, for the first time in seven years, Ella, Betsey, and I step out of the house . . . together.

There's a little shopping complex at the bottom of the hill boasting all the stores neighborhood residents could need or want. There's a small grocery store, a pizza place, an ice cream shop, a coffee hangout, a nail salon, a gift shop, a dog groomer, and a dry cleaner. Ella's driving, and she finds a spot in front of the least-frequented business—the reading-glasses store—and we all get out. Without words, we split up and walk to our destinations: Ella's in charge of pizza, Betsey will grab ice cream, and I'll stock up on toiletries.

I get what we need, pay, and leave the store, swinging the bags in my hands as I weave through parked cars. I breathe in the smell of pizza and environmentally friendly dry cleaning and feel at peace with things for the time being. Someone pulls into the space on the right side of the car, and even though they're parked way too close, I'm content to wait for the driver to get out.

Until I realize that the driver is Grayson.

"Hi, Elizabeth!" she says when she sees me standing there. "Sorry, let me get out of your way. I thought this space was bigger." She looks embarrassed as she shuts her door and has to squeeze between the cars to get out. "So, what's up?"

"Just getting groceries," I say, holding up my bags.

"Oh, cool," she says, glancing into the car. I do the same: Betsey and Ella are both purposefully looking away. "Who's that you're with?"

"Just—"

Beep! Ella lays on the horn at exactly the right moment.

"Some super impatient people, apparently," I say, laughing it off. "I guess I have to go. I'll see you next week."

"Okay, bye," Grayson says, looking confused but moving aside so I can get in. She waves and starts walking away.

"This was so freaking stupid," Ella says as I buckle my belt.

"She didn't see anything," I say.

But then, because apparently luck just isn't on our side today, there's a backup of cars leaving at the same time— right as Grayson makes it across the lot.

She has to walk in front of our car.

I hold my breath as she does, hoping she won't look over and notice us. She keeps her eyes ahead, but then once she's on the sidewalk on the other side and we start to creep forward, she glances at the car. Grayson sees me and smiles, then raises her hand to wave. But then her forehead creases.

"She's looking at me," Bet says through clenched, smiling teeth.

The car ahead of us moves. Ella floors it and almost hits a bicyclist, who swerves and shouts. I see in the side

144

mirror that the commotion pulls Grayson's attention away from us; she covers her mouth in surprise and pulls out her phone—probably in case she needs to call an ambulance. Thankfully, the guy's fine. But by the time Grayson looks at us again, all she can see is the backs of our heads.

"Freaking stupid," Ella says as we pull into traffic.

I turn around and look at Betsey, who seems like she might agree. Probably sensing my worry, she tries to lighten the mood.

"At least we got ice cream."

On the way home, we decide to wait and see what Grayson does at school. If she asks about it—which I hope she won't—we've got a story ready. If she doesn't, we're in the clear.

With Ella's "freaking stupid" comments all the way home, by the time we arrive, I don't feel like hanging out anymore. I take two pieces of pizza to my room and call Sean. As it rings, I worry about Mom seeing his number on the bill, but I ignore the thought in favor of Sean's voice.

"Lizzie B.," he says, like he's been waiting for me.

"Hey," I say, melting onto the bed.

"Hi," he says, and I can hear his smile through the phone. "I still have sand in my pockets."

"I still haven't washed my T-shirt," I admit, gripping the phone like it's a fish trying to squirm away from me.

"You look good in it," he says. "You should wear it every day."

"I'm not sure the others would go for that," I say, happy that I can talk about Ella and Betsey. Happy that he knows about them.

Sean and I are quiet for a couple of seconds, listening to each other's stillness. And then: "So, I have to talk to you about something," I say, remembering a conversation from earlier.

"Something *else*?" Sean asks, and even though he's joking, I can hear his nervousness. "Should I be worried?"

"I don't think it's that big of a deal, but you might."

"Why? What is it?"

"Well, you know that our mom will only let us date Dave," I say slowly.

"Yeah, but I sort of assumed..." Sean's words trail off. This is what I was afraid of: that he'd think I could simply start dating him instead. "You're going to keep seeing him, aren't you?" he says, voice dipped in jealousy.

"Well, it's not like I *like* him," I say. "But it's that or nothing. And dating *anyone* is a step in the right direction." I sigh. "Besides, it's not me who's dating him. I just have to tolerate him at school."

"You're not exactly selling me here, Lizzie," Sean says quietly.

"My...the others and I talked about it, and we think there's a way for us to date both of you at once."

"Won't your mom know?" he asks.

"Not if we're careful."

"I don't like this," Sean says. "What about at school

when you're with Dave? I'm just supposed to pretend I don't care when you're holding his hand in the hallway?"

"I don't hold his hand in the hallway."

"Ella probably does," he says.

I blow my hair out of my eyes, frustrated. Getting to know Sean shouldn't have to be this complicated. I don't answer because I don't know what to say.

"So, what are we doing then, Lizzie?" he asks seriously.

"I . . ." I begin. "I'm not sure." When I hear him tsk on the other end of the line, I hastily add, "But I know what I *want* to be doing."

"Okay," he says. "We'll figure it out."

"Will we?" I ask, feeling hopeful and defeated at the same time.

"Yeah," he says, surprising me by sounding sure. "We will."

sixteen

Monday at the switch, Betsey follows me outside to meet Ella. Even though it's lunchtime, she's still wearing pajamas. I hear her fuzzy slippers *shhshhshhshh* on the walkway behind me.

"What are you doing?" I ask, looking over my shoulder. She ignores me, so I turn forward again. I pull the bottom of my pink tank top so it's smooth under the white cardigan. I stop walking and wait for Ella to park, shifting my weight to my left foot. I hate these flats. Ella wears them all the time, but they pinch.

Ella takes her sweet time getting out of the car, but finally she appears. She flips her curly hair over one shoulder and starts toward us, removing the necklace and eyeballing Betsey at the same time.

"How was Grayson?" I ask. They have history together.

Ella shrugs. "Quiz day. She was late and I rushed out at the bell, so she didn't have the chance to say anything. I'm not sure she was going to, though."

Ella looks at Betsey. "What's up?" she asks, manicured eyebrows furrowed. It reminds me that I meant to pluck this morning. I hope no one notices that Elizabeth Best's eyebrows are less sculpted after lunch.

"Give me the locket," Bet says, holding out a hand.

"Why?" Ella asks, looking fearful, like she thinks Betsey might smash it or something. I gotta admit: I'm a little afraid myself. Betsey is getting pretty gutsy where Mom's concerned. She's seemed genuinely unfazed since Grayson saw us Saturday.

"Just do it," Betsey says impatiently. Just when I'm wondering whether Ella's going to refuse, she hands over the necklace, and Betsey quickly clasps it around her neck. Then Betsey looks at me.

"All she needs to hear is a heartbeat," she explains. "A calm, steady heartbeat. What's more calm than being at home all the time?" she asks with a smile, waving her right hand toward the house. "I'll just take it off when you're in dance, then put it back on for creative writing, and take it off again when you're at cheer. No problem."

"Except that if she logs on to the GPS tracking site

and finds that the necklace is at home, we're dead," Ella says.

Betsey shakes her head. "She won't. If there are no irregular heartbeats, no unexplained periods of time when the locket is silent, she'll have no reason to worry. No worry; no problem."

"What if she sees it on you?" I ask. "You're with her all afternoon."

"I'll hide it under my shirt," Betsey says. "Or I can pretend I'm cold and wear a scarf. I'll figure it out; don't worry about it!"

It makes sense, except Ella doesn't look convinced. I'm not sure I am, either, but I'm not about to second-guess the chance to spend an entire day without the possibility of being spied on.

"This is crazy," Ella says quietly.

"Being tagged is crazy," Betsey says. "This is very sane."

"She does it for our protection," Ella says.

"No," Betsey says, raising a palm and looking suddenly mad. "We live like we do for good reason, but the necklace isn't that. It's about her being absurdly overprotective and nothing more." Bet pauses a second, her eyes softening. She takes hold of Ella's hands. "El, is this what you want? To live a third of a life? To barely know what the world looks like at night?"

"To be banned from cheerleading just because you're good at trigonometry?" I add softly.

"But this is what we agreed to," Ella says. "It's just how things are."

"It's what we agreed to when we were too young to know better," Betsey says. "And it's not how it has to be."

Ella yanks her hands out of Betsey's, ripping herself from the truth.

"I'm not sure when you turned all Che on us, but I happen to be okay with my life," she says. "No matter what's up with Mom right now, the fact is that we don't have a fraction of the pressure that other girls our age have. Mom provides for us and basically leaves us alone. I'm dating Dave. We have everything we need. I'm satisfied, and I don't want you two messing it up." She exhales loudly. "I mean, first it's telling Sean, then all of us going out together and getting caught—it's all just too much. It's not worth it."

I bite my tongue instead of pointing out that she sounds like she's trying to convince herself. Her mention of Mom providing for us reminds me again that we have no idea how she's managing to do that. There's more to those twenty-thousand-dollar deposits; I just know it. But with Ella upset and the lunch hour dwindling, I choose to leave it alone for now.

"Let's talk about it later," I say to Ella, who shakes her head and goes inside. Betsey calls after her.

"Just don't say anything about the locket."

The day feels like one of those eggshell days from then on out, like things are going to crack if I bump them wrong. But then creative writing makes it all better. We have a sub, one who's clueless about the subject she's teaching and annoyed by the kids in class. So it's essentially a free period.

A free period with Sean.

Right after the bell, he turns in his seat to face me, moving in the direction of the wall so his back is to the rest of the class. We're in our own little bubble.

"Your hair is curly today," he observes, eyes playful.

"It is," I say, unconsciously grabbing a curl and twisting it. It's one of those perfect ringlets that I think looks good on everyone else, especially Ella. But this curly mane has never felt right on me. Sean scrunches up his eyebrows and looks me over one feature at a time. When I could swear he's staring at my nose, I ask, "What are you doing?"

"Just making sure..." he says. His eyes fall to my chin. He tilts his head to the side a little and purses his lips as his eyes dance down my arms all the way to my fingertips. "Yep."

"Yep what?" I ask, confused.

"Yep, it's you," he says confidently.

"How can you be so sure?" I tease. "We could be *Parent Trap*–ing you right now."

"You're not," he says, smiling.

"Seriously," I say, leaning forward. "I'm Betsey."

Sean leans forward, too, and we're almost inappropriately close for class. I can feel his breath on my lips. Without hesitation, he says, "You're Lizzie."

Smiling, I exhale and lean back again. "You seem pretty sure of yourself."

"About some things," he says, shrugging. Then: "About this."

We hold gazes for a moment. Loud laughter across the room makes us look away. When we've both checked it out—a guy fell out of his chair—we're back in our bubble.

"I got you a present," Sean says before leaning over to get something out of his bag.

"Oh, yeah? What is it?"

Under my desk, he passes something from his palm to mine. His fingertips touch my wrist at the transfer, and he might as well have just kissed my earlobe for the jolt it gives me. I move my hand to my lap and look down: It's a phone.

"It's prepaid, and only I have the number," Sean whispers. "Your mom won't be able to monitor when we talk to each other."

"No, she won't," I say, smiling with my whole face at him. I'll never have to worry about Mom checking the bill again. "This is spy stuff: You're pretty sneaky."

"And you're just pretty."

Sean scrunches up his nose at the line, but cheesy or not, I love it. And I love the way I feel when I'm near him, too.

Grayson looks at me quizzically at the start of cheer practice: I brace myself for the question I know is coming.

Then halfway through the hour, when everyone's going through a new cheer in small groups, she pulls me aside.

"Am I mental or do you have sisters who look just like you?" she asks.

I pause, probably a second too long, actually considering telling her. Now that we've told Sean, we can tell others, too, right? Then I snap out of it.

"You're mental!" I say, letting loose a laugh that I mean to sound breezy but doesn't at all. "Either that, or you need to have your eyes checked."

Grayson blinks at me; she's not buying it.

"I was with my cousins on Saturday," I explain. "Our moms are sisters, so some people say we look alike." I dramatically roll my eyes. "God, I hope not. You should see the nose on one of them. And the other is like a foot taller than me."

I force another laugh, and Grayson laughs politely herself, even though nothing's funny. Nothing at all.

"That makes sense," she says, probably thinking that it doesn't. But instead of saying anything more, she says simply, "Well, it was fun to bump into you anyway."

"You, too," I say.

We smile forced smiles at each other and she goes back to the front of the room to gather everyone. She eyes me suspiciously a few more times before practice lets out, but she keeps her mouth shut about the whole thing. I guess that's all I can really ask for.

seventeen

Life feels like one of Sean's pictures for two weeks: captured in a moment and standing still. I don't want to say *perfect*, because Mom and her secrets are always on my mind. I don't want to say *normal*, because that's not a word I know. So I'll say *steady*. Life is steady. But then it starts moving again.

Two weeks before Halloween, on a Thursday, Sean and I are parked in the lot of an abandoned superstore eating drive-thru tacos when I look down at my purse the second before it rings. I answer the call; it's Betsey.

"She wrote back," she whispers.

"What?" I say, plugging my left ear. "Who wrote back?"

"The girl from Twinner!" Bet says. "Her name's Petra and she lives in Oregon. And listen to this: She's *adopted*."

"Shut up," I say, allowing her enthusiasm to rub off on me. "I didn't really think it could be possible, but what if—"

"I know!" Bet whispers excitedly. "I mean, I didn't tell her anything really, but—"

Her words drop off. "Bet?"

"Shh!"

I glance at Sean, who's looking at me with amused curiosity. I realize then that I'm hunched over and clutching the phone like it's precious. Before I can say anything to him, Bet's back.

"I have to go," she says. "Mom's lurking around: I'm hiding in the closet. I'm going to write Petra back later and see if I can get more information out of her."

"Maybe you should become a detective when you grow up," I joke.

"Why do I have to wait until I grow up?" Betsey asks, laughing at herself. "Anyway, see you later."

I hang up, then relay the call to Sean.

"Does this mean that you're finally going to do something about it?" he asks.

"About what?" I ask.

He looks at me like I'm being an idiot. "Lizzie, your mom is borderline abusive—you get that, right?"

"Don't talk to me like I'm five," I snap. "And I know my mom...a lot better than you do. She may be one hundred and fifty percent overprotective, and she may have more than a touch of OCD, but she's not abusing us."

Sean sighs and scrunches up a taco wrapper.

"I think you have Stockholm syndrome," he mutters.

"I think you're making this more dramatic than it needs to be," I say. "I mean, yeah, I hate it. I want out of the arrangement as it stands. And yeah, my mom's wacked. But I'd appreciate you toning it down a bit."

"Just trying to help," Sean says.

"Well, stop."

"Fine." He's clearly annoyed. "But you said yourself, you get used to things to the point where they don't seem weird anymore. And you're used to this...but, Lizzie, believe me when I tell you: It's still weird."

"I get it, okay?" I say, looking out the window. "Can we just go back to school?"

He clenches his jaw and starts the car.

Barely anyone's around when Sean drops me off by the main entrance. Without words, he pulls away—he'll go to the student lot to park. I rush inside, feeling sick about our first fight, particularly because I know I'm the one who's wrong.

I shove my way through the swarm of students buzzing through the main hall. For the billionth time since we started at Woodbury, I wish that our assigned locker were in one of the less congested areas of the school. Sighing after someone elbows me in the back as she passes, I rush through the combination—3, 33, 13—wanting to just stash my books, get what I need for Spanish, and get out of here.

Dave makes sure that doesn't happen.

Usually, I don't see Dave at school, which is a good thing. Despite all of us knowing that he can't tell us apart, Ella still seems happy to be dating him, and even Betsey said he was funny after they went out for coffee when he just showed up as a surprise after night class. I'm the only one who's emotionally allergic to the guy. Which is, of course, why I'm the one he asks to the Halloween Dance today, of all days.

In the most humiliatingly public way possible.

I yank open the locker door and dozens and dozens of tennis balls come spilling out all over the main hall. The girl at the locker next to mine squeals and points at the ball avalanche, drawing even more attention to me and the situation. Since the hallway's so packed, everyone has to dodge the furry balls or risk tripping and falling: I get a seriously scary look when a girl wearing inappropriately tall heels nearly breaks her ankle trying to make it through the mess.

Almost in the same instant, I realize three things: Three of the balls are pink with words written on them; Dave and his friends are watching nearby; and approaching from the other direction is none other than Sean.

My real boyfriend.

The one who's already super mad at me right now.

Grayson and a girl I don't know are standing by their shared locker across the walkway. I look at Grayson, pleading with my eyes. Despite the fact that she probably still thinks I'm a liar, she smiles warmly and weaves through the crowd, bending to pick up balls as she approaches. By the time she makes it to my side of the hall, she's got an armload.

"Lily, will you go get a bag from the office?" Grayson calls over her shoulder.

"Sure," Lily says, slamming the locker and disappearing into the sea of people. I glance at Dave and catch one of his friends elbowing him on the arm in congratulations. It's annoying. Meanwhile, people continue to stare and laugh at the locker that vomited tennis balls and the girl desperately trying to contain them.

Whatever this is, it is not romantic.

"Thanks," I say to Grayson. "Guess he likes grand gestures." I nod toward Dave.

"Guess so," she says with a little laugh. Since the whole look-alike-cousin thing, there's been an invisible wedge between us, and it's not like we knew each other that well before.

"Aren't you going to read it?" she asks, pointing to a pink ball, then shifting to catch a yellow one that's trying to jump out of her arms.

"Oh, right," I say. One of the balls with a message written on it is right next to my left foot; I pick it up.

DAVE? is scrawled in black Sharpie across the fuzzy surface. Confused, I look through legs and feet for the other two. I see familiar shoes stop right next to me; Sean speaks.

"Looking for this?" he asks, holding out a pink tennis ball, the word DANCE written on it. Sean's face is neutral for the sake of the crowd, but his eyes are seething. And I get it: We just battled over my mom and now he's watching me get asked to a dance by another guy in front of the entire school.

I take the ball and glance at Dave, whose chest is puffed up like a rooster's. Sean follows my line of sight and shakes his head ever so slightly, then keeps moving down the hall toward his class. I want to chase after him, but I'm frozen. Thankfully, the warning bell rings, so the crowd thins. Grayson's locker mate, Lily, reappears with a massive garbage bag, and the three of us spend the remaining time gathering tennis balls.

"Thanks for your help, you guys," I say as I lean over to grab the last one.

"It's no big deal," Lily says, nodding to the bag. "Where do you want to put that?"

"I'll drop it off in the gym. I'm sure they can use them."

"Probably not this one," Grayson says, handing me the pink tennis ball that says WITH.

DANCE WITH DAVE?

As the final bell rings, I look over to where he was standing: He's gone. He made me, Grayson, and Lily late to class, but he didn't even stick around long enough to get my answer. God forbid he'd be late, too.

It was a gesture for the crowd that watched, not for Elizabeth Best.

Not for Ella.

Not for Betsey.

Not for me.

"I think we should break up with Dave," I say flatly during a commercial break that night. I haven't talked to Sean since our fight and I'm in a surly mood. We're eating ice cream in the rec room and Ella keeps looking over her shoulder, probably because we've been talking about Petra and Mom and Sean and other secrets, but it's bugging me. Everything's bugging me.

"Say what now?" Ella asks, even though she heard me. Her loaded spoon hangs in midair.

"I'm cool with whatever," Betsey says, leaning over and eating the ice cream from Ella's spoon.

"Sick," Ella says, scrunching her face in disgust.

"It was going to drip," Betsey says with a little laugh. "And besides, we probably have matching germs."

"I still don't want your spit on my spoon."

I roll my eyes at the two of them and the show comes back on; the matter is dropped. Or at least I think it is. A particularly tense scene starts and all of a sudden, Ella grabs the remote and presses Pause.

"Hey!" Betsey and I say in unison.

"We're not breaking up with Dave," she says to me, frowning. "I'm going to a high school dance!

"And you," she says, looking at Betsey. "Stop saying things like we have the same germs. We're not the same person!" Betsey laughs, which makes Ella frown deeper.

"I'm serious," Ella says quietly, which makes Betsey serious, too. "We may have matching DNA, but we don't like the same things. We don't make the same choices. We don't have the same dreams. We're our own people. I'm me. You're you. And Lizzie's..."

"From another planet," Betsey interrupts, making all of us laugh. Afterward, Bet grabs Ella's hand. "I know you're you. And I love you for you."

"I love you for you, too," Ella says. They hug, and I take the opportunity to eat the last bite of ice cream out of the container. The lump in my throat only makes it stick a little bit on the way down.

Later, I call Sean on the spy phone.

"Hey. I'm glad you called," he says when he picks up after the first ring. He sounds tired... and sad.

"Did I wake you up?" I ask.

"No," he says. "I was..." His words trail off and I feel like whatever he was doing when I called isn't important. It's this moment that matters. Sean sighs heavily. "Lizzie, I'm so sorry. I feel like crap about what I said. I can't believe I did that. It's none of my business."

"Yes, it is," I say forcefully. "I made it your business by

telling you. I think that I...I just don't know how to act sometimes now that you know. I mean, I know you're right."

"I just want you to have what you deserve: a real life," Sean says, and it makes tears pop into my eyes. "But it's selfishly motivated, too. I mean, I say those things for me. I want you to myself. I want to see you all the time, not just during the afternoons." He pauses. "When you're not around, I'm sad. It feels like something's missing. Like I want something I can't have."

"I feel that way, too," I say quietly.

There's a long pause, and I'm sure Sean's as confused as I am: He blows out his breath hard. So much needs to change before we can act like a normal couple: It feels like an impossible situation.

"I want to be the one to humiliate you in the main hall at school," he says.

"Funny." I bite my lip. "Hey, I'm really sorry about that."

"Not your fault," he says, but it sounds a little forced.

"Even so, I'm sorry you had to see it."

"Me, too." His voice is flat. "But I feel worse about our fight. It was a sucky day all around."

"Not all of it."

"No?"

"I can think of at least one redeeming moment."

"Oh, yeah?" he asks, his tone softer. "What's that?"

I want to talk things through with him; I want to figure

things out together. But there's been so much weighing on me—on us—that I take the chance to lighten the mood.

"Have you forgotten about the kiss in the drive-thru line?" I ask, remembering spontaneously leaning across the gearshift and planting one on him. Remembering the way he sucked in his breath in surprise when my lips first touched his—it gave me shivers.

"Mmm," he says in a tone that does it again. He sighs contentedly this time. "Yeah, you're right. That kiss in the drive-thru line saved the day."

eighteen

"She joked about us being related," Betsey whispers at breakfast.

"Why are you whispering?" Ella asks. "Mom's vacuuming. Can't you hear it?" I listen to the rhythmic roar of the vacuum going back and forth over the carpet in one of the bedrooms upstairs. My guess is that it's Ella's.

"Oh, right," Betsey says. "Anyway, I joked back that we were separated at birth, and I asked where she was born. I'm hoping all this joking will lead to some serious info."

I swallow a bite of melon. Then, with Sean's words in my head, I say, "I think we need to figure this out, and if it turns out that she's the Original, we confront Mom once and for all."

"And if she freaks out?" Bet asks.

"Then she freaks out," I say. "It's not like I'm saying we should go to the police and get her in trouble. But we deserve to know what's going on."

"Why not just ask her now?" Betsey asks.

"Well, if Petra's really Beth, I'd rather know going into the conversation," I say. "Wouldn't you guys?" I wait for two heads to nod in agreement before continuing. "Anyway, Bet, I'm sure you can figure it out relatively soon. We can wait another couple of weeks."

"And then we demand answers," Bet says. I nod, and we both look at Ella.

"Are you in?" I ask, thinking she'll say no. Instead, she surprises me.

"Yeah, I'm in."

At the switch, Ella's late *and* she tells me there's no gas in the car. I can feel a mood radiating from her; something must have happened at school.

"Why didn't you stop?" I ask.

"I did it last time," she says, with a little too much sass. I roll my eyes.

"What's with you?" I ask.

"Nothing," she says. "Just…Dave was weird today. Sorry. I'll fill it up next time."

"It's okay," I say, giving her a quick hug before jogging to the car. I've got to hurry or I'll be late to Spanish.

I cruise down the hill, music blaring, to the closest gas

station. Luckily, there's no one else filling up. I pull in so the pump's on the right and hop out with purpose. Then I remember that the gas tank is on the left. Sighing, I climb behind the wheel again and back out, then pull around to the other side so the pump's on the left. An older red BMW pulls into my former spot.

I want to check my phone, but I've read the Internet warnings about being set on fire while tweeting, so I just lean against the sedan, watch the numbers creep up, and breathe in the smell of gasoline. I seem to have gotten one of those pumps that don't have a "high" setting, and I'm growing more stressed about being late by the penny.

"Nice day, huh?" a voice says. I look over and see that the driver of the BMW is smiling at me. She's got blond hair, is about my mom's age, and looks a little familiar. She's wearing a gray business suit and trendy big sunglasses and I wonder if I've seen her on a real estate sign or something. Her look screams *salesperson*.

"Sure," I say, glancing at the blue sky and thinking that it should be illegal to comment on the weather in San Diego. I look at the slow-moving numbers on the pump and wonder if I should stop it, then start again to see if it'll go faster.

"Do you go to Woodbury?" the woman asks, gesturing toward school.

"Uh-huh," I say. "I'm on lunch break."

The woman nods, then tips her head to the side. "You look familiar," she says. "Do you live in Mira Mesa?"

"No, up in the hills," I say, waving in the general direction of my house. After a lifetime of being taught to fear strangers, I don't get too specific.

"I'm Mary," she says. "What's your name?"

"Uh..." I say, looking down and toward my car. I don't want to tell her my real name, but right now I can't think of a single other name in the world. Then, finally, I say, "Natasha."

"Nice to meet you, Natasha," the woman says, smiling in a funny way. I have no good reason to think this, but I don't believe that her name's Mary. Then again, I just told her I'm Natasha, of all people.

The pump keeps crawling and the lady keeps gabbing. I try the stop-and-restart thing; it doesn't work.

"So, are you from here?" she asks.

"We moved here when I was nine," I say, seriously considering just going to school and letting Betsey deal with gas later.

"Where did you move from?" Mary—or whoever she is—asks. Just as I'm formulating another lie in my brain, the gas tank goes clink. Relieved, I reach over and pull out the nozzle, and replace it in its holder. The screen asks me if I want a receipt; I punch the No button.

"Sorry," I say to Nosy Mary, "I'm late for school."

"Have a good day...Natasha," she says.

I get into the car and buckle up, then drive around past the woman's side of the island to leave the gas station. I'm not sure what makes me look over but I do: The little computer on her side is stuck on the welcome screen. I think back to when she arrived: Did I hear the beeps when she punched in her selections, or did I just assume she was getting gas because she put the nozzle in her car?

More important than what I remember, though, is this: If she wasn't actually getting gas, then what was she doing?

nineteen

I look over my shoulder for a couple of days, but when I don't see Nosy Mary again, I call the enounter random and move on. By the night of the Halloween Dance, I've all but forgotten about my awkward conversation with the strange lady at the gas station.

Betsey and I help Ella get ready for the dance. With two dryers to make it go faster, we each take half of her head and diffuse dry her curls. Then Bet and I each hold one side of the yellowing strapless dress we got on eBay while Ella steps in. I feel like a forest animal helping Cinderella, but Cinderella's ball gown was a lot cleaner.

With a black ribbon that hits the smallest part of Ella's waist, her dress was probably pretty once. But then it sat in someone's closet for a few years, and once in our hands, it was tossed in the dirt and intentionally slashed to serve as the perfect outfit for a Zombie Prom Queen.

"You look so creepy," I say, smiling.

"She doesn't even have on her makeup yet," Betsey says devilishly. "Wait until she's got exposed brains on her forehead."

"Just don't make it too gross," Ella says. "I don't want to turn off Dave."

"Not possible," Bet says. "That dress may be old, but it was made for you. He's going to drool, exposed brains or not."

At eight o'clock, Bet and I are reading in the rec room when my spy phone rings. I glance at Betsey and she smiles, but doesn't take her eyes off the page.

"Hello?" I say quietly.

"Hi there, Lizzie B.," Sean says in a tone so low I can barely hear him.

"Why are you whispering?" I ask, sitting up on the couch, because I think my voice sounds weird when I'm lying down.

"I'm just...I don't want anyone to hear me."

"Where are you?" I ask curiously.

"On your front porch."

Panicked and overjoyed at the same time, I throw down the phone and jump off the couch.

"What's happening?" Betsey says, looking at me funny.

171

"Sean's here," I say as I run out of the room. I race down the stairs, skidding around the landing in the middle, and rush to the front door. When I fling it open, there's no one on the porch.

"Hey!" I whisper into the darkness. "Sean?"

"Hi," he whispers from somewhere to my left. "Is your mom here?"

"Now you ask me that?" I say, stepping out onto the porch and looking in the direction of his voice. I see him standing in the bushes, smiling. His hair's not stuck up in its usual style tonight; instead it looks like he put his chin down and shook his head hard and his hair stayed that way. There are shiny pieces crisscrossing each other on his forehead, threatening to conceal his eyes. But thankfully, they don't. He's so gorgeous in the moonlight.

"Surprise," he says.

"You're insane," I say, rolling my eyes at him despite feeling overjoyed to see him. "Get in here." He gently climbs out of the bushes and carefully wipes his feet on the doormat, then steps inside. He kicks off his shoes without me asking. He's wearing holiday-appropriate orange-and-black-striped socks that I find adorable on him. He stands there, holding his shoes in one hand and his bag in the other, just looking at me.

"Hey," he says seriously. There aren't any lights on in the entryway; we're shadows.

"Hi," I say.

"I'm really sorry for being a jerk this week," he whispers. "I mostly came over to tell you that."

"You weren't a jerk," I say. "You were just...upset. I can see how you would be. I know it can't be easy to have Dave—"

Sean steps so close to me that our noses could touch.

"I was a jerk," he says. "And I'm sorry."

A wave of emotion rolls through me; I just nod once so I don't cry or anything embarrassing like that. I turn toward the steps.

"Let's go up." I wave for him to follow me. His sweet apology still floating in the air like bubbles, I walk softly up the edge of the stairs for fear that my footfalls will ruin it. Maybe feeling the same way, Sean's quiet behind me. But when we get to the top of the stairs, Betsey shouts a loud hello.

Pop.

We head into the rec room.

"Look what I found in the bushes," I say, smiling. Bet laughs.

"Did you take some ballsy pills tonight, Sean?" she asks.

He laughs as he sits down on the couch opposite Betsey. He sets his bag next to him; I want to ask what's in it, but I decide to wait until we're alone.

"I figured that if I couldn't take Lizzie to the dance, I'd bring it to her."

"That's barfingly cute," Betsey says. "Later, lovebirds." She stands and leaves. I blush a little at the "lovebirds" comment, but Sean doesn't seem to mind.

I sit on the couch next to him, and just as I open my mouth to ask about the bag, he speaks first.

"Is your mom going to be home soon?" he asks.

"No. At least I don't think so." Automatically, I glance at the doorway.

"Should we go to your room?"

"What?" I ask, blushing full-out this time, which makes Sean look away, embarrassed.

"I didn't mean it like that," he says. "I was just trying to think of a place we could talk where your mom wouldn't immediately see us if she came home."

"There's only one room in the house she'd never barge in," I say.

"Which one?"

"The bathroom."

I make Sean sit on my bed while I toss makeup, eyebrow wax, and tampons into the basket under the sink. When I've hidden all my junk, I grab two pillows from the bed and prop them against the wall under the towel rack, between the vanity and the glass shower stall. I'm actually thankful for my mom's obsessive cleanliness: The floor in here is spotless. I light the vanilla candle on the toilet tank and flip off the light, then let Sean in. Once he's settled, I make sure my bedroom door is shut, then I shut and lock the bathroom door, too. I sit next to Sean closest to the shower.

"This might be the weirdest date I've ever had," he says, shifting a little to get comfortable on the tile floor.

"It's for sure the weirdest one I've ever had," I say, thinking that so far, most of my dates have been pretty strange.

"Well, it's about to get weirder," he says before grabbing and unzipping his bag. He pulls out a small box and hands it to me. "Can't have an exclusive Bathroom Halloween Dance without a corsage," he says when he sees my confused look. I open the box and think at first I'm seeing black roses. Then I realize that it's dark chocolate.

"You can eat it." He laughs a little, like he can't believe he's giving me a chocolate corsage.

"It's the best of both worlds," I say, pulling it out of the box and putting it on my wrist. My cheeks pinch as I try to fight off the biggest smile ever, as I attempt to remain calm. I lean over and take a bite. "It's both beautiful and delicious!" I chew a chocolate petal. "Want some?"

I hold up my left wrist; Sean takes my hand and my forearm gently in his hands and lifts the corsage to his lips. He takes a bite, eyes on mine, and I'm zapped. We stare at each other for so long that I feel it in every inch of me. I'm sure he's going to kiss me, but instead, he retrieves from his Date-in-a-Bag several other items, including a long black Elvira wig for me, a seventies Beatles wig for him, several black plastic spider rings, two sets of vampire teeth, Waldo and Wenda hats, and an iPod and a mini speaker station.

He plugs in the mobile sound system and pulls me to my feet. We both put on our disguises and then he gently takes me in his arms. There in my candlelit bathroom, in the space between the toilet and the vanity, me looking like Goth Undead Wenda in Pajamas and him dressed as Ironic Vampire Teen Ringo Starr, I share my first dance with a guy.

. And as weird as it is, it's perfect.

twenty

"How was the dance?" Mom asks at breakfast the next day.

"So fun," Ella says, stars in her eyes. She looks how I feel.

"That's nice," Mom says. "What time did you get home?"

"Eleven," Ella replies. Mom eyes her skeptically. "Fine, twelve."

Really, I'm probably the only one who knows that Ella sauntered in closer to one. It was long after Bet went to bed. I only know because it was then that I was walking Sean up to the gate, laughing at his dramatic story of how he scaled it like a pro before he called me from the front porch.

Betsey was right: He really did take some ballsy pills last night.

I drop my chin so Mom won't notice my giddiness.

Mom asks about the decorations and the other kids' costumes, and while Ella describes everything in detail, I am horrified to hear a noise from upstairs. Our communal cell is on the counter behind Mom; the spy phone in my bedroom is ringing.

I look at Ella; she notices it, too. I see a flash of panic in her eyes before she blinks it away. Slowly, she stands with her still half-full plate and walks through the kitchen, still talking. Mom interrupts.

"Ella, you need to finish your eggs, at least," she says, eyes following her. Then, "I think your phone's ringing." Just when Mom starts to look at the spot where we usually plug in our cell—where it is, in fact, plugged in right now—Betsey squeals.

"Oh my god!" she says. Mom jumps and looks at Betsey, surprised.

"What?" Mom asks.

"There's a mouse!" Betsey shouts, pointing in the direction of the living room, away from the phone. While Mom looks for the rodent Ella takes the opportunity to grab the phone and shove it in her pants pocket. I sigh quietly, relieved.

"Where?" Mom says, staring wide-eyed in the direction Bet pointed.

"It was right over...oh." Betsey fakes embarrassment. "Whoops."

"What?" Mom says. "What now?"

"I think it was just Lizzie's fuzzy slipper."

"For goodness' sake, Betsey, you scared me!" Mom says.

"I really thought it was a mouse," Bet says, shrugging.

Mom joins Ella at the sink. "Now that that's settled, I'm going out to get groceries before work. Anyone want to come?" She looks at us individually, expectantly. I feel guilty for not wanting to go, and impatient for her to leave. Ella agrees to ride along; Betsey tells Ella to bring her back a latte; and I manage to stay downstairs until the door shuts behind Mom. Then I race up to my bedroom.

"My mom almost found out about the spy phone!" I say the second Sean answers. I'm a ball of nervous energy.

"No way," Sean says. "Sorry about that."

"It rang up here when our real phone was plugged in downstairs," I say. "Close one. We have to be careful."

"Totally. Sorry."

"No worries," I say. "So, what're you doing today?"

"That's actually why I was calling," he says. "I was wondering if you wanted to come over and hang out this afternoon. You know, after your mom leaves for work." He pauses a second. "I'm sure my mom would love to meet you."

"You told your mom about me?"

"Of course," Sean says easily. Sometimes it shocks me how grown-up he seems: He's not intimidated by or embarrassed about anything like a lot of the other guys at school. Compared to David, Sean's a man.

"That's really sweet," I say softly.

"Thanks," he says, and we both get quiet. Then: "I mean, I didn't tell her everything. I didn't tell her about Ella and Betsey, even though I really still think that we should do some—"

"Sean?" I interrupt.

"Yeah?"

"I'll come over if you promise not to bring that up again," I say, flirty with seriousness mixed in.

"Okay," he says. "I promise I won't mention your mom or your living arrangements ... today."

"Okay," I say. "See you in a few hours."

As I breeze through a yellow light, I rethink the long-sleeved tunic, skinny jeans, and flats that I'm wearing. Ella said it worked, but now I wonder if Sean's mom will think I'm trying too hard. I mean, I look like I'm in a catalog. And not only that, but I straightened my hair *and* added a single braid across the top and down the right side. I grab the tiny rubber band at the end of the braid and start to tug until I realize that taking it out now will leave me with a weird crimpy section of hair. I can't meet Sean's mom as a one-sided frizz-head, so I leave it in.

The sedan's GPS directs me to Sean's neighborhood and his house. I hold my breath as I park in front of an older home with a pitched roof and massive, funky numbers over the front door. It's muted green with white trim and has a small, manicured front lawn.

I get out and lock the car, then make my way up the

front steps to the porch. I ring the bell and wait, turning a little to look out toward the neighborhood. Sean lives in University City, so there are a lot of younger people out; it must be fun to live here.

The door opens and I turn around, expecting Sean. Instead, it's a woman I assume is his mom.

"Hello!" she says with a wide, welcoming smile. "You must be Lizzie."

I nod and extend a hand; she looks surprised, but she shakes it anyway. Her hands are small, but her handshake is firm. She smiles with light brown eyes that match Sean's, but her hair is long and blond and she looks like she's in her thirties even though she's probably at least a decade older. She's beautiful, and I can see parts of Sean in her face.

"Nice to meet you, Ms. Kelly," I say, before realizing that because she's divorced, she might have a different last name.

"Call me Harper," she says, which confuses me even more. Is that her last name or her first? And where the heck is...

"Hey, you," Sean says, walking up behind me onto the porch. "Sorry, I was moving my car so you could park in front."

"Thanks," I say, smiling at him.

"Come on in, you two," Harper (or Ms. Harper) says. Sean leads and I follow. The front door opens right into the living room: There's no entry or grand staircase, just an open space with a TV and couch on one side and a

181

dining table on the other. Through a door, I can see a kitchen; I assume the bedrooms are through the other visible opening. It's a small, older home, but it is beautiful and perfectly...calming.

"Welcome," Harper says, waving her hands around the space. "Make yourself at home. I'm making cookies.... I'll be right back."

She turns and disappears. I look around, wishing I could live somewhere like this. The floor is wide wood strips stained light gray, and the walls in the main room are painted a pale butter yellow. All the trim and built-in bookshelves are white, and the oversized sectional couch is dark charcoal gray. There are sheer white coverings on the wide windows, and someone with a scratchy voice is singing from the first actual record player I've seen in real life. A tiny hot dog scampers across the floor.

"I didn't know you have a dog," I say.

"I never told you about Dumptruck?" he asks.

"That miniature dog's name is Dumptruck?" I ask in disbelief. Sean nods. "It's kind of perfect," I admit with a laugh as I watch Dumptruck try to hop up on a chair in the sun. Sean walks over and gives him a boost, then returns and kicks his sneakers into a pile by the door. He's wearing one orange and one navy-blue sock today, which makes my stomach flip.

I step out of my shoes and wiggle my toes, wishing I'd worn socks. Going barefoot on a first visit feels funny. And besides, it's a little chilly today. As if he's reading my mind, Sean asks, "Want me to grab you a pair of socks?"

"Is that weird?" I ask.

"Not at all. Follow me."

He leads me by the hand through the doorway off the dining area. There's a long hallway with several open doors on either side; we walk all the way to the end, passing what Sean points out as Harper's room, an office, a spare bedroom, a single bathroom, and finally, his "lair."

It's sparse and incredibly neat. The walls are stark white with white wood detail on them. There's a mattress and box spring on the floor in the corner covered with a solid navy-blue quilt. Next to the bed is a low industrial metal nightstand; there are a desk and a shelf made out of the same material on the far wall. The desk is tidy, with an older laptop hooked to a flat-screen monitor and several binders stacked to the side. The bookshelf looks like it was once organized, but now books are lying horizontally on top of the vertical stacks.

"You need a bigger shelf," I observe.

"Yeah, but I like that one," Sean says, walking to the far wall and opening a door. His closet is neat, too. He pulls striped socks out of one of those hanging organizer things.

"Is your room always this clean?" I ask, looking around.

"Would it freak you out if I said yes?" he asks, grinning while offering me the socks.

"Not at all," I say, taking the socks and sitting down to put them on. They're black and yellow like a honeybee and way too big for me, but something about wearing them feels nice. "School spirit," I say about the colors.

"Go, team," Sean says sarcastically.

"Oh, hey," I say in a whisper, glancing at the door. "What's your mom's first name?"

"Harper," he says in a matching whisper. "Why? Did you think that was her last name?"

"Yes!" I say, laughing loudly, which makes Sean laugh, too.

"Don't worry, everyone does," he says. "Her last name is Kelly, just like mine."

"Your parents didn't give you your dad's name?"

"No, thank god," Sean says, rolling his eyes.

"What is it?" I ask, standing and moving so I'm right in front of him.

"Not telling," he says in a low, sexy voice.

"Come on," I say, "I told you I'm a clone. The least you can do is tell me your dad's last name."

"Hooker," he says flatly.

"Did you just call me a hooker?" I joke.

He shakes his head at me but doesn't answer.

"Your name would have been Sean *Hooker*?" I ask, biting my cheek so I don't burst out laughing.

Sean nods. "I don't know why he never changed it," he says. "But that's not my problem anymore." His tone is serious; my smile fades. Wanting to take his mind off bad memories, I lean up on tiptoe and kiss him gently on the lips. He smells like outside.

"Thanks for having me over," I say before I kiss him again. "And thanks for the socks."

"Anytime," he says, leaning in. Just then, his mom calls "Cookies are done!" from down the hall, and we jump apart like startled cats. Sean smiles sheepishly and nods in the direction of the door; I float down the hall behind him, loving the feel of my toes inside his striped socks.

After snacks and some pleasant parental conversation, Sean and I go back to the living room and sink into the couch. I scratch Dumptruck while Sean texts back one of his friends. When he's done, he takes a picture of me with his camera phone.

"Let me see it," I say, grabbing the phone. "I have to approve it."

"You always look good in pictures," he says.

"Not true."

"No, really," he says. "You do. Hey, want to go see the studio?"

"Yes!" I say enthusiastically.

At the shoe pile by the front door, Sean digs through a few strays until he finds what he's looking for: hideous green foam shoes. I make a face.

"What? Dislike?" he asks with a little laugh.

"Why do you own those?" I ask, frowning. "You look...I mean...they're the worst."

"I know," he says, laughing again. "They're hot. I'm going to wear them to school on Monday."

"No!" I say. "You'll be banned!"

I shove my own feet into my flats even though I'm still wearing the oversized socks. The extra material bunches up at the sides and makes my feet look like I'm retaining massive amounts of water.

"I guess we both look like fashion don'ts," I say.

"Great, let's go." He takes my hand and leads me out of the house, carefully closing the door behind us so Dump-truck doesn't get out.

"They're for cooking," Sean says as we walk down the steps.

"What's for cooking?"

"My shoes. Cooking requires long periods of standing up. These are comfortable when I cook." He leads me around the side of the house and to the back toward a detached garage.

"They're still hideous," I say, shaking my head, wondering whether I like him more for liking to cook or for having special shoes to do it.

"All the famous chefs wear them." Sean opens the people door next to the double garage door and waves me through.

"Hideous," I say with one last look at his feet. "I mean, seriously, why—"

Sean pulls me close and kisses me sweetly right there in the doorway. "Shh," he says, lips still pressed against mine. His face pulls back an inch but his arms hold me tight. I feel him doing something with his feet, then he gets a little shorter like he just kicked off his shoes. Our bodies still stuck like Velcro, Sean pats my right leg. "Lift up your leg." I do, and he worms his toes into the heel of my shoe so it pops off. Then somehow without looking, he kicks his shoe under me in the right direction. "Step in," he says. He goes through the same process with the other foot, all while maintaining the hug hold. Finally, when I'm in shoes and he's not, he pulls his face back another inch and raises his eyebrows at me.

"So?" he asks.

I roll my eyes dramatically, Ella-style.

"Fine," I say. "They're comfortable."

Inside the garage, I immediately forget that I'm in a garage. Walls have been constructed to divide the space, and everything is finished and painted; it's heated, warm, and inviting. We walk into the front reception area, where the floor has bright carpet tiles in every color and the walls are covered floor to ceiling with massive framed photos: students, babies, people getting married, land-scapes, animals.

"Is that you?" I ask, pointing to a gigantic shot of a smiling, chubby baby in a basket.

"No," Sean says, looking embarrassed.

"Liar," I say, turning to inspect the photos on the wall by the door.

"Your mom's insanely good," I say, admiring a close-up of the wrinkles on an old man's face. "Wow," I murmur. "I love this." I reach out but don't touch a portrait of Dumptruck.

My eyes travel up the wall; I jump when I recognize my own face staring back at me. It's a close-up and my dark eyes are huge; my hair is blown back like I'm a model. It's beautiful and cringe-worthy at the same time.

"That's my favorite one," Sean says, walking up behind me.

"It's really..." I say, my voice trailing off, not sure how to express how I feel. Instead, I say something else. "It's nice of your mom to let you hang it in her studio."

"Yeah," Sean says. "That's my wall."

I turn around, wide-eyed. "You took all of these photos?" I ask. He nods. I turn to look at them again; they're even better now that I know they're his.

"They're beyond amazing," I say, feeling like it's too small a compliment. I hear Sean's stocking feet shuffle once; I wiggle my toes in his too-large shoes.

"Come see the rest," he says, grabbing my hand and literally pulling me away from his art.

We walk through another door into a massive open studio with umbrella lights and a tripod and several stations that look like mini rooms that forgot some of their walls. There's a five-by-five section of dark hardwood floor with patterned frilly wallpaper on the wall; one with a white floor and a blue painted wall; and one with a brown wood floor and three solid canvas backdrops to choose from. There's a changing room in one corner blocked off from the rest by thick fabric; in another corner there are baskets of props ranging from silly glasses to masks to toys to tutus.

Sean and I spend an hour messing around in the studio:

him taking photos of me and using a little remote to take photos of us together, and me shooting mostly unfocused pictures of him. It's so ridiculously fun that I lose track of time. When Harper appears in the doorway asking if I'd like to stay for dinner, I panic for a second before remembering Mom's at work. Still, I don't want to overstay my welcome.

"I should probably get home," I say. Who knows if Bet needs to go somewhere; I'm eating into evening.

"Oh, that's too bad," Harper says. "Maybe some other time."

"Definitely," I say, hoping it's true. Harper is the definition of what a mom should be; what does that make my own?

"Well, it was really nice to meet you, Lizzie," she says. "I hope you'll come over again soon."

"I will," I promise. "Thanks for the cookies."

Harper leaves, and Sean and I linger in the studio a little longer.

"Your mom's so nice," I say. "And *sane*."

Sean wraps his arms around me and looks into my eyes. "I promised I wouldn't touch this particular subject today, but if you really think your mom's got issues, you should seriously tell someone," he says. "I mean, it doesn't have to be someone...official." He pauses. "We could just tell...like maybe my mom?"

"Don't," I say quickly, stiffening. "I don't want to... just don't." I take a deep breath. "Not yet, anyway."

I still feel like I need answers before I can ask my mom any questions—and that the questions should come from our family and not the outside world.

"Do you really have to leave?" Sean asks. "'Cause I was thinking pizza sounded good."

"Isn't your mom making dinner?" I ask.

"She won't mind," he says, shrugging. "She was probably planning on ordering pizza anyway; I'll bring her some back."

"Let me call Betsey and make sure it's okay that I'm still out," I say. When Sean looks at me funny, I smile half heartedly. "This is her time, not mine."

Bet's cool, and Harper seems to love the idea of pizza, so Sean and I set out to get food. We take my car, because his is parked in a good spot; he tells me directions to a pizza place in University City.

"We can't go to my favorite place; Dave works there," I say.

"Ah, the dreaded Dave," Sean says. "Did Ella have fun at the dance?"

"I think so," I say. "I haven't had much chance to talk to her about it."

"Did you have fun at the dance?" he asks, looking over at me before adjusting the music dial.

"The most fun ever," I say honestly. "Thank you."

We're pulling into the lot of the pizza place when my cell rings.

"Get back here!" Ella whispers. "Mom's home!"

"Oh my *god*!" I shout. A car honks behind me because I've just stopped driving in the middle of the road. I pull forward and to the side. "Why?"

"I have no idea," Ella says. "I'm hiding in your bathroom. I ran up here when we heard the gate opening and saw that it was her. Bet's downstairs—she told her that I went out for ice cream with Dave."

"Oh my god!" I say again. "She'll know."

"No, she won't; just act like me when you get home. And besides, you're the one who's all about taking risks lately. Wasn't it you who said, 'Mom's lying, too, so who cares?'"

"It's different when I'm the only one who's going to get yelled at," I say, blowing out my breath. "But I guess if she recognizes me, then tonight's the night."

"Okay," Ella says. "If I hear trouble, I'll come down. If nothing happens, I'll sleep in your bedroom and you sleep in mine."

"Okay," I say, feeling sick about the plan.

We hang up and I update Sean, who looks a little too excited by the prospect of everything coming out. "It's going to be fine," he says. "Want me to go with you?"

"No!" I say. "That'll make it even worse."

He opens the door and starts to get out.

"Where are you going?" I ask.

He smiles warmly. "I'll take the bus back home," he says. "I need to get pizza for my mom, and you should go face the music. I think you'll feel better afterward."

"I hope you're right."

Sean leans back into the car and kisses me on the cheek. "I'm right," he says before turning and walking away.

My stomach is in knots the whole way back up the hill. When I pull off the main road, I stop before I get to the gate to calm myself. There's another car idling down the secluded lane; it's probably one of our neighbors, and I'm sure they're wondering what it is I'm doing.

I let the possible conversation play out in my mind:

Where have you been?

Out with a friend. Where have you been every night for the past . . . forever?

What do you mean?

Mom, I know about your office. I know you're not a doctor. Where is that twenty grand coming from every month? And what do you do at night? Oh, and PS, is the Original still alive?

"Okay," I say to myself in the rearview mirror. I take a deep breath and blow it out. "You can do this."

I put the car into drive and cruise down the driveway, then park in our usual spot. I don't waste any time getting out and heading inside; I don't want to lose my nerve.

In the entryway, I stand alone, listening. Waiting. There's a TV on in the rec room; the foyer and dining room are dim. I can tell from the glow through the doorway that only the under-cabinet lights are on: Nobody's in the kitchen.

Tentatively, I kick off my flats. I turn and lock the front door as quietly as I can. Then, holding my breath, I tiptoe up the stairs. I peek around the corner to the rec room; no one's there, but there's a soda on the table and a book face-down on the arm of one of the couches. I turn and look down the hall; Mom's bedroom light is on, but her door's closed. In about four strides, I slip into Ella's room, carefully shutting the door behind me. I jump when the phone buzzes in my hand. The caller ID says Home; it must be Ella. I answer without saying hello.

"You made it," she whispers.

"I did."

"Okay, change into pj's; I'll come to my room and we can switch. Your bed sucks."

I laugh quietly. "See you in a sec."

My heart is still racing: I feel like Mom's going to step out of the shadows at any moment. I inch my way to Ella's closet in the dark and step inside, turning on the light only when the door's closed. Hastily, I change into sweats and a T-shirt, leaving my clothes in a crumpled mess on the floor. When I'm searching for socks, the closet door opens.

"It's just me," Ella says, palms up. "Sorry."

"I think I just had a heart attack," I say, sighing. Then, "What the hell is she doing home?"

"I have no idea," she says, taking off my favorite sleep T-shirt while I hand over hers. "Bet came in after they talked and she said Mom was acting really weird. Asking what we did today. I guess she asked when I was going to be home like three times."

"Maybe she knows we know," I say.

"Or maybe she knows about Sean and she's checking up on us."

"This is getting insane," I say, grabbing a rubber band from a hook and tying back my hair like Ella's. "I mean, she's starting to act like a prison warden, don't you think?"

Ella just shrugs, but it's weak. I know she agrees with me.

"Sean thinks we should tell someone," I say.

"Like who? The police or something?"

"I think he meant his mom, but just someone," I say. "He's worried about us."

"Are you sure he's not just interested in seeing you more often?" Ella says. It comes off as a little defensive; she changes the subject. "Oh, hey, Bet said that Petra scanned some of her baby pictures. I guess it's freakish how much she looked like us. She said she sent her school picture, too."

"Bet seems pretty positive that she's Beth," I say.

"I don't think she's positive," Ella says. "I think she just sort of *wants* her to be the Original. But it's so weird: I mean, how did she end up with different parents...in Portland? Even though she looks just like us, I'm not completely sold. I think the only way we could ever know for sure is a DNA test."

"How would we even do that?" I ask.

"Online," Ella says like it's nothing. "You swab your cheek and they'll tell you if you're a sibling match."

"But we're not si—"

Ella and I freeze when we hear someone come into her room.

"Bet?" she mouths to me. I shrug. We both watch the handle on the closet door turn. I glance down at what I'm wearing; I look like me. And thankfully so, because the next thing I know, Mom's standing in the doorway.

"Oh, good, you're home," Mom says to Ella. She glances at me, then looks back at El. "What are you two doing in here?"

"Just planning our outfits for the week," Ella says casually. She turns and pulls a miniskirt off its hanger. "I like this better with the shirt you picked out," she says to me.

"Fine," I say. "I'll give you the skirt if we can wear jeans with the blue sweater."

Mom shakes her head at us and laughs. It's no different from the way she's always laughed, but knowing what I do about the double life she's leading, it sounds...off. I want to ask what she's doing home tonight, but I don't want to spend more time with her than I have to. I hold back.

"I'll leave you two to your planning," she says, turning away. But before she leaves, she looks back at Ella. "Have fun tonight?"

"Sure," El says, smiling.

"What flavor did you get?" Mom asks, like the answer is somehow important.

"Mint chip," Ella says without missing a beat. I'm amazed at her skills as an actress. Mom nods, looks at both of us one more time, and turns and leaves.

"Good night," she says before closing the door to Ella's room. El and I look at each other wordlessly for a few long seconds. Then, after we're sure Mom's out of sight, I creep back to my bedroom, secrets still safe.

What I realize when I'm alone in my room is that I can't decide whether I'm happy or sad about it.

twenty-one

Monday after school, the carpet is being cleaned in the commons, so cheer practice is cancelled. Time on my hands, I wander slowly from my locker to the parking lot. Sean's hanging out with his guy friends, who have, apparently, complained about him being MIA lately. When I'm nearly to my car, someone calls my name. I turn to see Alison from dance waving at me.

"Hi, Alison!" I call. She hurries over, her shoulder bag smacking her on the hip as she walks. "What's up?"

"Nothing much, just headed home," she says. "How about you? Why aren't you at cheer practice?"

"Cancelled due to carpet decontamination," I say. She

laughs. "Honestly, it's nice to have the break. Dance was brutal today; I'm wrecked."

"Same here," she says, brushing her red hair out of her lip gloss. "I was thinking of stopping for coffee on the way home; I could use some downtime before seeing my family. You want?"

I cock my head to the side, considering. Mom doesn't know cheer was cancelled, and Bet doesn't need to leave for a while yet. I'm surprised to find myself able to say, "Yes, actually, that sounds great!"

Alison and I drive separate cars to a nearby coffee shop. At one point, I swear I see the red BMW that Mary woman drives behind me, but when I look again, it's gone. Alison and I park in spaces next to each other, go inside, and order matching drinks. We and our skinny vanilla lattes settle into cushy seats by the window. We chat about dance and classes and how Principal Cowell seems to wear the same sport jacket every third day, and it's just . . . easy. I never knew friendships could be like this.

When it's getting toward Betsey's time of the day, I tell Alison I need to get going. She nods, then looks at me seriously.

"Lizzie, you and Dave aren't together anymore, are you?"

"What?" I say, caught off guard by the abrupt topic change.

"Dave Chancellor?" she says. "I mean, I know you went to the dance together, but you're not still into him, right?"

I never was.

"Uh, yeah...I am," I say. "We're still together. Why?"

Alison's eyes widen, then she frowns with purpose. "Listen, this is going to sound really weird, but I feel like we're, like...friends...even though we haven't hung out before today or anything."

"I feel the same," I say, smiling. "And I'm just over-subscribed. I'd love to do this again. It's been really fun."

"I agree," she says, shifting like she's suddenly uncomfortable.

"What is it?" I ask.

"So, because I feel like we're friends, I want to tell you something," she says. "But it's...I feel bad about it. It's bad."

"Just tell me," I say, my stomach knotting together.

Alison leans forward, hugging her arms to her chest, looking at me like she's genuinely concerned and not just gossiping as she says what she wants to say. Her mannerisms tell me that she's a good person. That despite the blow she delivered, I'm leaving the coffee shop with a new friend. A real friend.

And for that reason, I'm only half on fire on the way home.

After a lot of back and forth, it's decided that it'll be me.

On Tuesday after the switch, I crank up angry-girl rock on my way to school, singing along with the lyrics as loudly as I can. I can't get over the fact that Dave cheated on Ella—he was the one who pursued her in the first place! And with Morgan, of all people! I shake my head, turn the music up louder, and press down on the accelerator, pissed and determined to protect Ella's heart.

I storm into school, pausing at the top of the two steps that drop down into the packed cafeteria to scan the crowd. I easily spot Sean, who raises his chin at me with a sexy smile on his lips...until he sees the expression on my face. Then he looks worried.

He watches me search for Dave.

Surrounded by fellow football players, Dave's eating french fries and laughing like nothing can touch him. Well, maybe nothing can, but I'm about to do my best.

I take one step down, then two, eyes on Dave. I walk straight down the middle of the aisle cutting the two sides of the cafeteria, slow and deliberate. In the periphery, I see a few students look up at me; it could be my imagination, but it feels like some of the chatter tapers off, too. Dave's at the last table on the right and Sean's at the second table in from the center, middle row, left. Thankfully, Dave is facing in my direction, so he sees me approaching.

He smiles at first, a cocky *come here, baby* sort of smile, but then he, too, looks worried when I don't smile back. The memory of Ella's tears eggs me on and forces me to swallow my nerves. When I'm even with Sean's row, eyes still on Dave, I turn and make my way toward my real boyfriend. I stop right behind Sean; he spins around on the bench and asks conspiratorially, "What's going on?"

"Just go with it," I whisper, pulling him up.

When Sean's standing, I step so close to him that I hear a few chuckles from his table. And then there are a few more when I pull him close and kiss him hard, long, and lingering, like I do when we're alone. In this beehive swarming with activity, I'm not sure that many people see the kiss, but I hope that Dave does. That's all that matters.

When I step back, Sean's grinning like it's his birthday, but he doesn't say anything. He just watches me walk back to the center aisle, then make my way to Dave's table. I know immediately that he saw me kiss Sean: His face is red; his jaw is clenched. Loudly, from a few feet away, I say what Ella wouldn't have been able to.

"So, obviously, we're over. Enjoy Morgan."

I tell Grayson I need to go home for a family thing after school, but instead I meet Sean in the parking lot. He's leaning against the trunk of the sedan, waiting for me. In distressed jeans, a gray hoodie, and dark sunglasses, with his hair stretching to the sky and his eyes on his phone, he's gorgeous.

"Hey, you," I say sweetly. He looks up and smiles.

"There you are," he says. "Feel like going back to the cove?"

"Seems fitting," I say, remembering our trip there after I told him I'm a clone. It only seems natural that we'd go again on our first day as an official couple.

Sean has to stop first at the post office to mail some photos for his mom. It sounds weird, but the normalness of running errands with him warms me. We take Sean's car because mine's almost out of gas, and when we're out on the main roads, he cranks up the music and we both sing out of tune.

"What's going on with that Petra girl?" Sean asks when the song's over.

"Betsey set up a time to talk to her on the phone this weekend," I say. "She's going to try to see if there's a good time to ask if she wants to do a DNA test."

"I'd like to be a fly on the wall for that conversation," Sean says, laughing. "I like Airborne Toxic, too; want to take a DNA test to see if we're related?"

"I know; me, too," I say. "But Bet will figure out a way to ask her."

We chat through the commercials about nothing, then The Bravery comes on. He turns it up again.

"I love this song," I say.

"I love you."

It's so nonchalant—his eyes still on the road—that it takes a second to hit me. When it does, I suck in my breath and look sharply at him. Feeling my stare, he smiles, but keeps his eyes on the road. I look away and roll down my window a little, because suddenly I feel hot. We get caught at a light and when he stops, he looks at me.

"Lizzie," he says. I look at him.

"I heard you," I say, smiling.

"Yeah, but it came out wrong," he says. "I think about

it all the time—I think about you all the time—and it just came out sort of . . . light. But I mean it."

I have to look away from his intensity: I glance at the stoplight to make sure it's still red.

"Lizzie," he says again, drawing me back in. He touches my right jawline with three fingertips. "I've never said it to anyone else, but I know what I feel. I'm completely serious when I say that I love you."

Beep.

Beep, beep.

Hooooonk!

I know the light's turned green; I know the other drivers are mad. But I don't tell him to move. Instead, I say:

"I love you, too."

At the post office, Sean parks in the spot farthest from the door and then reaches back and grabs a box. He opens his door, then looks at me.

"Wanna wait here or come in?"

"Let's go."

The line is long and narrow; Sean stands behind me with a hand on my hip, whispering weird things into my ear to pass the time.

"Do you think Ella and Betsey will fall in love with me, too, since you did?"

"Don't flatter yourself," I say, laughing. "You're not *that* awesome."

"Funny," he says. "Hmm...I wonder if the Original will inexplicably fall in love with me, too?"

I roll my eyes, not justifying that one with an answer.

"Hey, what if your mom lied about there being an Original and she just cloned herself?"

"We don't really look like her," I whisper.

"What if you're a clone of a famous person?" he says quietly.

"You've lost it," I say a little too loudly; the surly postal worker gives me a look. I turn around and smack Sean, because we both know it was his fault.

Finally it's our turn and of course the mean lady is the one who helps us. She says a total of five words through the whole painful transaction. When we're finished, we grab hands and rush away from the counter. Sean heads toward the IN door instead of the OUT; I yank him in the right direction.

"Can you actually *read*?" I joke as we step outside.

I'm watching Sean laugh instead of looking where I'm going when I almost bump into someone.

"*Elizabeth Violet Best!*" a voice hisses.

And that voice belongs to my mother.

I'm completely quiet the entire ride home, and for the duration of the twenty-minute "conversation" I have with Mom once we arrive. When it's nearly over, when I'm ready to just hear my punishment and go hide in my room, Mom notices that I'm not wearing the necklace. She screams at Ella and Betsey to come to the living room, then tells all three of us that we're grounded.

"What did we do?" Ella asks, looking her most innocent.

Mom narrows her eyes at her. "You three live one life; if Lizzie's stepping out of line, you all know about it. You're accomplices."

"That's crap," Betsey says.

"I see you're wearing the necklace when Lizzie should be," Mom counters. Betsey shuts up. For some reason—maybe it's because we all want to believe we're on the brink of something with Petra and want to see how it plays out—none of us mentions that we know about Mom's secret life.

"So, what does that mean, exactly?" Ella asks in true Ella style. She wants ground rules.

Mom looks at Betsey, "First, it means that you will quit your job. There's no reason for it other than an opportunity to socialize and make spending money for clothes and music, which you will not be purchasing anytime soon." Betsey's shoulders slump. "You'll continue with night class," Mom says.

My stomach seizes up the second before she narrows her eyes at me.

"And Lizzie, here's what being grounded means to you," she says. I brace myself for losing the car, being forced to take the bus. What she says next never enters my mind. "Ella is taking school full-day."

"What?" I shout. "You're not letting me go to *school*?"

"Oh my god," Ella groans. Now she has to go back to cheer practice with Morgan, the boyfriend thief.

"That's right," Mom says, crossing her arms over her chest, almost like she's proud that she's hit a nerve. "Until after Thanksgiving holiday, Lizzie is completely housebound. If I catch her out of the house, the time is extended."

At this point, she's not even looking at me. Everyone's quiet, wondering if there'll be more or if that's the end of it. Finally, after seemingly millions of ticks of the clock, Betsey asks, "Can we go?"

Mom nods. We three move toward the doorway, but before we're in the clear, she speaks again.

"Oh, and I'm taking your cell phone, too."

I've never been angrier in my life: I feel like I could scream down buildings or throw a car or cause a tornado if I was allowed out of the house. I know Ella and Betsey are just as mad as I am, and it's probably making me madder. I can feel their rage mixing with mine and turning all three of us black inside.

As much as I've deceived Mom, it's nothing compared to what she's doing to us. I pace like a lion in a cage, and consider confronting her with what I know. Then I realize that doing so right now will only make it worse. I'm trapped in the house: She can easily lie to me and extend my punishment. And this weekend, Betsey will talk to Petra. So instead of saying anything, I vow to find out what's going on once and for all.

I decide that it's time to take back my life.

twenty-two

The second day of my punishment, Mom moves my computer to the kitchen island. She announces that she'll be changing the password daily, and I can only use it for two hours for homework when she's there to supervise my online time. Three-plus weeks of my prison sentence ahead of me, when she actually looks over my shoulder as I Google a vocabulary word, I shove back and tell her that I'm boycotting homeschool.

"It's not like it matters," I say. "Ella's the one getting the *real* grades."

"That's your choice," Mom says, talking to me from the entryway as I storm up the stairs. "But for every assignment you fail to complete for homeschool, you add another half day to your punishment."

I continue up the stairs and slam my bedroom door so hard it rocks the house. But later, I finish the assignment. I may be fraught with lava-hot fury right now, but I'm not a moron.

I'm not about to add to my sentence.

"Are you all right?" Sean asks the third night; we're on the spy phone, my last remaining link to the outside world. Mom's at work, but I wouldn't put it past her to come home to check on me, so I'm on the floor of my bathroom with the door locked and the fan going.

"I'm a prisoner," I groan. "It's not like I was really all that free to begin with, but this is ridiculous. I mean, I can take missing school. I can handle being without my computer...mostly. But..." I'm quiet.

"I'm so sorry," he says. "Does it make you feel any better to know that I'm miserable without you?"

"A little," I say, smiling weakly.

"Just a little?" he asks. "Come on."

I laugh out loud, and the jolt of it makes the tears I've held back fall from my eyes. Suddenly, I'm laughing and crying at the same time. "I miss you," I say when I catch my breath.

"I miss you, too."

I wipe away my tears and sniff loudly; there's a break in the conversation before Sean speaks again.

"Lizzie, I know you don't want to talk about this, but I really think we should tell someone," he says gently. "I'll talk to my mom; I'll tell her not to do anything about it without your permission. I just feel like someone needs to know. She might have some good advice."

"No, Sean, don't," I say forcefully. "Really. I'm serious."

He huffs. "Are you seriously going to keep defending her? Saying that she gave up so much for you? I mean, for god's sake, you're locked in your house."

"I'm fully aware of where I am," I say, growing angry. "But if someone outside our family is the one to call Mom on her shit, she'll freak and possibly *move* us again. Do you want that?" I'm glad for the fan at the end; my voice is loud.

"Of course I don't want that," he says in a gentler tone. "But I want you to be safe. At first, it was just the schedule. Then the dating. Now you actually can't leave the house. I'm afraid for you; I'm afraid of what's next."

"She'd never hurt us," I say. "She honestly believes she's protecting us."

"From what?" Sean asks.

I'm quiet for a few seconds. "I'm not sure at this point," I say finally. "All I know is that Betsey, Ella, and I need to be the ones to confront her directly. And if we can do it with a DNA test that says we know the Original is alive, plus the address of her secret office and the knowledge that she doesn't work at the hospital, we've got so much proof that there's no way she can lie anymore."

"And then what?" he asks, sounding worn down. "What will come of it?"

"I've been thinking about that," I say. "I think if it comes down to it, we need to trade our silence for identities."

"You're going to blackmail your mom?"

"Sean, you're the one who's always pushing me to get out of this situation," I say. "I mean, we'll try to reason with her. But if it doesn't work—if she won't listen—then yeah. We might just have to scare her into freeing us."

The eighth day, I'm in the rec room watching TV when I see out of the corner of my eye Mom go into my room with a laundry basket. I could help her—my room's a disaster area—but instead, I turn up the volume and scrunch lower into the couch.

Two hours later, when I decide to change out of sweats, I walk into a room that barely looks like mine. The clothes are gone from the floor; the bed is made hotel perfectly; the curtains are drawn and the window is open. My vanilla candle is lit on my desk and it smells so nice. I smile for maybe the first time since I saw Mom outside the post office, wondering if this is her version of a peace treaty.

But then I walk into the bathroom and see an empty tampon box on the vanity, and I know without checking for sure: She found the spy phone.

My connection to Sean is gone.

twenty-three

When Mom goes out on Saturday, Betsey, Ella, and I run to my room. Bet dials the number scrawled on a piece of scrap paper and sits down on the desk chair. Like kids at story time, Ella and I sit cross-legged at her feet. We hear the cell ring once, twice, three times....

"Hello?"

"Petra?" Betsey says. "It's Betsey. From Twinner?"

"Oh, hi!" the girl says. Everyone around me has the same voice, so I could be wrong, but hers sounds a lot like ours. "How are you?"

"I'm okay," Bet says. "Just hanging out. How about you?"

"I'm good," Petra says. "But I thought you were going

to call a little earlier. I might have to cut this short; I'm headed out to a birthday party."

"Oh, cool," Betsey says, and I can hear in her voice that she's disappointed. "Yeah, sorry for not calling earlier. I was doing some stuff for my mom...you know, your long-lost mother." Betsey fakes a laugh and I hear one on the other end of the line.

"She's probably better than my *real* birth mom," Petra says.

"You know her?" Betsey asks. Ella and I look at each other excitedly.

"I've never met her," the girl says. "I just have this whole made-up persona in my mind. In my imagination, she had me as a teen and was way too young to handle a kid, so her parents made her give me up."

I feel sad for her in that moment: having to make up the backstory to her own life.

"Anyway, I've gotta go," she says. "I can't be late to my own party."

"Oh, it's your birthday?" Betsey says.

"Well, not until next week, but yeah, it's my party," she says. "Sweet sixteen."

"Well, happy birthday," Bet says, "and maybe I'll call you in a few days." Bet missed it, but Ella heard: I know because her face looks as disappointed as I feel.

"Okay, great!" Petra says. "Have a good afternoon. Bye!"

Bet hangs up and looks at us: It's not until then that she notices our expressions.

"What?" she asks.

"You really didn't hear what she said?" Ella asks. "Betsey, she's sixteen."

The realization visibly registers; Betsey slumps in the chair.

"But she's a senior," she says. "She looks older than us. And she sent me her senior picture. How can she be younger than us?"

"I don't know," I say. "Maybe she skipped ahead—you said she's really smart. And you're right, she does look older. But you don't need to call her back. If she's younger, there's no way she's Beth. I guess..."

Ella sighs hard and finishes my thought. "It's over."

twenty-four

It was only one of several secrets, but for some reason, taking the Original out of the equation also takes the wind from my sails. I guess in some way I was starting to hold out hope: Hope that there was someone sort of like family out there in the world. Hope that if she was living a normal life, we could, too. But all that this exercise with Petra did was remind me of cold, hard reality. I was created in a lab from a dead girl's DNA. I was created *illegally*, and because of that, I am destined to be hidden.

For a full forty-eight hours, I stay in bed. I fall into an abyss of depression, not eating, not sleeping, not answering when Sean goes so far as calling the landline, ignoring Ella and Betsey when they ask if I'm okay. Staring at Mom like I can see through her when she comes in to get laundry. Then Monday evening, the others pull me out of it.

I'm lying on my bed, staring at the bugs in my light fixture, commiserating with them because they're trapped, too, when Ella comes in and flops down next to me.

"Have you actually been wearing that shirt for three days?" she asks.

"Four," I mutter, still looking at the bugs.

"You're sort of disgusting," she says with a small laugh that I don't reciprocate.

"No reason not to be," I say.

"Well, actually, yeah, there is," she says, rolling to her side and propping her head in her hand. "Bet's got class tonight and Mom's gone, and I set it up with Sean today. You're riding along and hanging out with him on campus until class is over."

I turn my head so sharply I think I pull a muscle in my neck.

"No way," I say. "Mom would go ballistic if she found out. I'm just stuck here in this cage."

"No, you're not," Ella says. "And she won't find out. Now come on, I don't like seeing you like this." She pauses before adding, "I don't like smelling you like this."

This time, I actually do laugh a little.

"Lizzie?" she says seriously. I raise my eyebrows at her. "Bet and I have been talking a lot about what to do since that whole thing with Petra. We're fed up, and we need answers. We decided the best time to do it would be

Thanksgiving holiday, when Mom's home from work... whatever work is to her."

"The best time to do what?" I ask.

"Break into that office and see once and for all what she's doing there," Ella says. My eyes widen; I mean, I've thought of doing it, but coming from Ella, it's like permission. "One of us will make up a reason to be out of the house, and the other two will keep Mom distracted while the first one breaks in."

"I'm going," I say.

"Since you know where the office is and have Sean to help you, that would obviously make the most sense," Ella says, "but you're grounded. She'll never let you leave."

I can feel the fire returning to my belly; I sit up straight on my bed.

"Then I won't leave," I say. "You or Betsey will."

"Me," Ella says definitively, getting it. "You're better at pretending to be me."

I shower and Ella helps me flat iron my hair, then Bet and I take off with me lying down in the back of the sedan just in case Mom's out on the roads somewhere.

"Ella told me you want to be the one to do it," Betsey says as she makes a left.

"Yeah," I say. "I've been to the office, so I won't waste any time getting there. Plus... I don't know: I sort of feel like I started all of this. Like I should be the one who ends it."

"Mom started it," Betsey says, "but I get what you're

saying. It's fine by me." Bet pauses for a second. "In fact, I've got the whole thing choreographed in my mind."

"I can't wait to hear all about it," I say, laughing.

"Later," Bet says, turning up the country music. "They're playing my song."

When we pull up to the college, Sean's lounging on the steps of the redbrick classroom building. He's looking at his phone and doesn't see us, but when Bet goes over and points out where I am, he stands quickly and puts the phone away. Feeling like I haven't seen him forever, I'm as nervous as that first night at the football game when he starts walking in my direction. His hair's shaggy tonight without styling products, and he's wearing a dark thermal shirt that's fitted but not too tight. He's got a light jacket on, and halfway across the lot, he stuffs his hands in his pockets and looks down and away.

It's the first time I've ever seen Sean look nervous.

But when he reaches the car, when he gets in the backseat next to me, when he turns toward me and I can see how much he's missed me, the nervousness is gone. We crash hard into each other and kiss like we haven't seen each other in years, not days, his hand winding in my hair and my arms gripping tight around his neck. I don't think about how much I hate my mother; my only thought is that I love, love, love this guy.

When a rent-a-cop circles the parking lot for the third time, Sean and I decide to get out and walk the campus grounds. I lock the sedan and Sean takes my hand; we walk onto a dimly lit path around a little pond.

"I'm really sorry things didn't work out with that Petra girl," he says quietly. "I know you were hoping they would."

"It's okay," I say. "Really, I'm not sure what I was hoping for. Just . . . something."

"Answers?" Sean says. I shrug. "I mean, if I were you, I'd want answers. Your life is so . . . strange. It'd be easy to get caught up in wanting to know where you came from. All you have is what your mom's told you, but now, knowing that she's lying about a lot of stuff, it's probably easy to think she lied about that, too. I can see why you wanted to believe that Petra was the Original."

I feel a swell of emotion for Sean and his ability to see me—to know me—without explanation. I love Betsey's and Ella's support—we're all in this together—but when it comes down to it, Sean's keeping me sane.

"I guess it's hard to know where you're going when you have no idea where you came from," I say.

"Yeah," Sean says. "I can see that. But Lizzie? You're so strong: You'll be fine. Whatever happens, you're going to be okay."

I stop walking and face him. "Hey," I say, grabbing his arm so he stops, too. He turns and brushes a stray piece of hair out of my eyes. I think of how before I met Sean and saw what real life looked like, I was actually okay with my situation. It's like he held up a mirror in front of me and I didn't like what I saw.

"I'm glad you're in my life," I say.

Sean wraps me in a hug and murmurs in my ear.

"I'll stay as long as you let me."

By the time Betsey's class is over, Sean's up to speed on the break-in plan and has a list of items to get to help with the mission, ranging from the practical, like his camera, to the somewhat ridiculous, like a laser pointer.

"Why on earth would we need a laser pointer?" I ask.

"I have no idea," Sean says, "but it just seems cool to have one."

I giggle to myself about how when I first met Sean, I thought he looked like an off-duty superhero; now I think that sometimes he acts like one, too.

He walks me back to the car and kisses me once more just before Betsey emerges from the building.

"Oh, hey, I almost forgot, I brought you a replacement spy phone." He turns and jogs to his car, retrieves a package, and jogs back.

"Thanks," I say, taking the paper bag from him. "I guess I'll have to find a better hiding spot."

"Yeah, well," he says, half smiling. "I brought you three more, just in case."

When Betsey and I pull off the main road and stop at the gate, we're still excitedly talking over each other about the office break-in plan and what we might hope to find.

Betsey jokes about Mom being a janitor while I type in the code and wait for the gate to open. I take my foot off the brake and start easing down the driveway, and just as I do, I notice a car parked down the lane like the time after Sean's when I came home because Mom was here. The car is obscured by trees before I have time to mention it to Betsey, but for some reason, it bugs me long into the night.

twenty-five

A little over a week later, I wake up like I've been shot with adrenaline. Today's the day. At some point in the next twelve hours, I'm going to break into my mother's office and discover what she's been hiding. Then Betsey, Ella, and I will confront her at last. Everyone's home from school and "work" for Thanksgiving break, and we have five whole days ahead of us to hash things out.

Today's the day we get our lives back.

The only thing is that we're not exactly sure when or how to do it.

The idea is that one of us will find a reason to go out. Our last-resort scenario is that at Mom's busiest moment—like when she has her hands in a turkey—Betsey will say she needs Advil for cramps and is too sick to drive. I, as Ella, will volunteer to go out, then we'll all pray like hell Mom buys the switch.

It's weak, but after going through what felt like hundreds of even weaker options, we decided it was the best. But I think all three of us are hoping that some better opportunity will naturally present itself.

Betsey, Ella, and I congregate in the rec room after breakfast. Mom's awake but in her office downstairs; I haven't seen her yet this morning. Ella turns on the TV; none of us watches. Instead, we three spend the passing minutes giving one another meaningful glances. Waiting for something to happen. I'm dressed in Ella's favorite cardigan and flats, and Ella's wearing my new captivity uniform: faded jeans and a gray hoodie. She has stick-straight hair and her legs are folded under her; she's sitting on my side of the couch.

Because I'm facing the hallway, I see Mom in the doorway before the others do. My anger pumps through my veins, but I shove it away, thinking: *What would Ella do?*

"Hi, Mom," I say brightly. She smiles.

"Good morning, girls."

I glance at Ella, who's deliberately not looking at Mom. She's scowling, and on her face, I see the me I've become.

"I'm going to shower and then head out to brave the grocery store," Mom says. "Our turkey is ready for pickup and I need to get everything else before the lines are too long. Anyone want to come?"

"I'm in the middle of a book," I say, patting the hardcover on the side table next to me. "Sorry."

I could be wrong, but I think I glimpse something funny in Mom's eyes, like maybe she's not buying it. But instead of asking me why I'm wearing Ella's clothes, she looks at Betsey.

"I have cramps," Bet groans, setting us up nicely for the Hail Mary scenario in case we need it later. Finally, Mom's eyes fall on Ella.

I hold my breath.

"I don't suppose you'd like to join me, would you, Lizzie?"

Ella doesn't flinch, but I have to bite the inside of my cheek to keep from beaming: It worked!

When Ella remains quiet for a few more seconds, Mom rolls her eyes. "I see," she says. "Well, then, I'll go take my shower. You three enjoy your show."

"Can we play Jenga later?" I ask, just to seal the deal. Ella loves Jenga.

"Of course," Mom says, smiling again before turning and walking down the hall to her room. When her door is closed, Betsey springs up from the couch and runs downstairs. In two minutes, she's back.

"What are you doing?" Ella asks. Betsey holds up two shiny keys—one silver and one gold.

"Making your life easier," she says to me. "These are the only two keys on Mom's keychain that I don't recognize. One of them has to open the office."

"What if she notices?"

"Wouldn't you rather take the chance than have to break a window or something?" Bet asks.

"Yeah, I guess you're right," I say. "So when am I going? When she's back?"

"No!" Betsey says in a low tone. "This is even better. You're going to leave when she does. She'll never know any of us left the house."

"But what if she comes back before I do?" I ask. "We won't know when she's on her way home. Ella can't go with her, and you just said you have cramps."

"Oh," Betsey says, as if she didn't think of that.

"Call Sean," Ella says evenly. "He loves this stuff, and he loves you. He'll totally follow Mom." She glances at the closed door at the end of the hallway. "But do it soon: You know how fast she gets ready."

My conversation with Sean is quick and efficient. He's up for anything, including staking out my mom. He's only seen her that one time at the post office, so with just a few minutes left, Betsey logs on to the computer and sends a photo to his phone. We all take our places in the rec room again until Mom leaves, then after we hear the gate close, I dash to my room and grab two of the spy phones. I use one to call the other, then hand the one I called to Ella.

"Now you have the number on the ID," I say.

"Good thinking," she replies. "Okay, you need to go...like now."

I run down the stairs and out the door with Bet and Ella trailing behind me.

"Call us with updates," Bet says.

"Be careful," Ella shouts.

"Okay," I say to both of them before throwing myself behind the wheel and starting the car. I head up the driveway and through the gate, then down the hill, biting my bottom lip all the way.

I'm parking on the street about a block away from Mom's office when Sean calls.

"She's here at the store," he says quietly. "I've got her."

"Okay, great," I say. "Remember to stay out of sight. She might remember you."

"So?" he asks. "There's no law against grocery shopping."

"I guess you're right," I say. "Sorry." Deep breath. "All right, I'm going in."

I walk up the steps to the office that just has to hold all the answers. I'm not sure what makes me try the silver key first—I guess I just like silver better than gold—but it works. I'm half expecting an alarm to wail or someone to jump out at me when I open the door, but almost more terrifyingly, nothing happens.

I step inside and breathe in through my nose. The place has that metallic antiseptic smell to it like a dentist's office. There's a vacant reception desk and a doorway leading to a hallway; I walk through and turn left: the direction that Mom came from that day I saw her here. There's an office at the end of the hall.

When I go in, I gasp.

Three walls are covered in corkboard and pinned with photos and notes. It looks like what you'd expect in the office of someone tracking a Mafia family. Except that the photos on the walls aren't of criminals: They're of me, Ella, and Betsey.

I take a step closer to the wall I quickly see is mine. There are tons of notes scrawled on yellow legal paper, but one in particular catches my eye: *Tendency toward fight (vs. flight)— Sympathetic Nervous System difference when compared to #1 and #2.*

I step over to Ella's wall; the phone rings and I jump.

"You scared the hell out of me!" I say.

"Sorry," Sean says, laughing a little. "Just making sure you're okay. Are you in?"

"I'm in."

"And?" I feel like he's holding his breath.

"It's...I don't know," I say. "It's an office with walls of photos of me, Betsey, and Ella, with a ton of notes. It's like she's monitoring us, only she *lives* with us. And most of it is really stupid stuff." I take a step closer to the photos of Ella. "Like, okay, here's an example: There's a note pinned here about how much sleep Ella gets. Apparently she averages eight point two hours per night."

"What the...?"

"I don't know," I say, moving along the wall. I notice that there are pictures of the palms of our baby hands, and fingerprints with little circles on them to show the patterns. I look from Ella's to mine; they look the same to my untrained eye. "It's like we're her . . . project."

"You said she was a scientist," Sean says. "Do you think she's like studying you or someth—"

"Oh my god!" I say loudly. I'm back in front of my wall, and in the corner, there's a hazy black-and-white picture of Sean and me leaving his house.

"What?" he asks, concerned. "Is everything okay?"

"She knows about us," I say flatly. "She probably knows everything." I let the thought sink in, and after a few seconds, I start to feel okay with it. She knows and she's let it go on. She must have a reason: Maybe it's that deep down, she does want me to be happy.

"I don't know about you, but I think that's a good thing," Sean says.

"I think it is," I say quietly, smiling. "Hey, let me call you back. I need two hands to snoop."

Sean laughs. "Okay, I'll keep an eye on the mark and call you if anything changes."

"You've been playing too many detective video games," I say, laughing, too. Then, "Thanks, Sean."

"You know it."

We hang up and I linger on my wall for a while longer, then start going through papers on my mom's desk. There are three stacks of more photos and notes—maybe things she hasn't gotten around to hanging up yet—and halfway through the second one, I see a photo of a woman I recognize: the one from the gas station.

Nosy Mary.

It's a professional photo like you'd use on a business card, printed in black and white from the Internet on regular multipurpose paper. There's a phone number but no name written in the white margin; it's unclear whether the number and the photo are related.

I consider calling the number until suddenly I remember thinking I saw Nosy Mary's car when I got coffee with Alison. It dawns on me that maybe Mary's a private investigator or something, paid by Mom to follow her own children.

My ringtone startles me; I drop the photo and answer the phone.

"Hi," I say.

"Your mom left the store," Sean says urgently. "She was in line to pay and she got a call and then just rushed out of the store. She abandoned her cart. At first, I didn't follow....I thought she'd left her wallet in the car or something, but then I saw her driving away. I ran out and followed her.... She's going in the direction of your house."

"How close?" I say, stepping toward the office door.

"Too close," Sean says. "You'll never make it back in time. I'm sorry I didn't call sooner, but I was gunning it, trying to catch up with her."

I'm quiet for a few seconds, considering. Then I sigh. "Well, if I'm caught out of the house anyway, I might as well get all the ammo I can. I'm going to need it." Pause. "I'll call you right back; I'm going to call Ella and Bet to warn them."

From my recent calls, I redial the other spy phone, but no one picks up. I weigh the downside of having this number show up on the bill for the landline and decide that by the time the bill comes, this will all be over. I call, but no one answers there, either. I call Sean back.

"What do you want me to do now?" he asks.

"Just make sure she goes home," I say. "Then I guess you're off duty."

"No problem."

Sean and I stay on the phone while he drives, me telling him about the pictures and notes on the walls and him commenting on my mother's utter strangeness, until he reports that Mom is turning off the main road to our house.

"Just go by," I say, my heart sinking, thinking of Ella and Betsey having to try to tap dance out of this situation all alone. It bugs me that they haven't called back yet.

"Stay on the phone with me, okay?" I say. Having Sean in my ear now is like a down comforter in the dark: It's security. Sean agrees, then launches into a story about the woman who'd been in line behind Mom at the grocery store—apparently she had a total meltdown about the abandoned cart. I open my mouth to say something when suddenly, without an ounce of warning, the most electrically charged surge of panic runs through me.

I suck in my breath and put my hand to my chest as my heart rate skyrockets, seemingly without cause.

"Lizzie, what's wrong?" Sean asks. "Are you okay?"

"I...can't...breathe..." I say through gasps.

"What?" he asks. "Are you serious? What happened? Did you touch something weird that maybe...Are you allergic to something?"

"No," I say, gasping. "Nothing."

"Can you sit down?" he asks. "Put your head between your knees?" He waits a beat and then says, "I'm coming there. I'm coming to get you. Screw your mom; you need to go to the hospital."

"N..." I try, but I don't have enough air to say the word. My ribcage feels like it's sealed in a concrete mold. "No," I say. "I...need to...calm..."

Sean gets it and his tone evens out. "Shh, Lizzie, just breathe," he says into the phone. "Put your hand on your heart; imagine that it's mine. I'm here for you. You're okay; just breathe."

I hear a car honk; I picture him flipping an illegal U-turn to come and help me.

"Breathe with me," he says before taking a deep inhale, then exhaling. My palm is still firmly on my chest—not pressing, but resolutely planted there. I pretend it's his.

"Take a breath," Sean says before inhaling and exhaling again. Once more, and my heartbeat starts to slow. Another time, and I start to breathe with him. A few more breaths, and I'm back to normal.

"Whoa," I say when I can talk again. Only then do I realize I'm on the floor of my mom's office. I start to stand up but feel woozy, so I stay put for now.

"What happened?" he asks.

"I don't know," I say. "It felt like a panic attack or something. I have no idea why...." My voice trails off; I'm preoccupied by the fact that even though I'm breathing normally now, I'm still feeling very unsettled. I'm jumpy. I snap my head in the direction of the doorway. No one's there.

"What's happening?" Sean asks, sounding worried.

"I don't know," I repeat. "I'm...I wonder if someone saw me come here?"

"Your mom's going to find out soon enough, right?"

"I guess, but...I just have this weird feeling right now. It's like suddenly, I'm...*afraid*. Not of Mom, but of something...."

"There's nothing to be afraid of," he says sweetly. "You're totally safe."

That's when it hits me.

"I have to go," I say urgently.

"What now?" Sean asks. "What's happening? Are you all right?"

"I'm fine," I say. "But I get it now. I may be safe, but the others aren't. Ella and Betsey are in trouble."

I call home five times on the way, but no one answers.

"Please be okay," I say out loud, feeling strongly that something is seriously wrong. "You have to be okay."

I go through it in my mind as I drive. Sean said that Mom got a call, that she abandoned her shopping cart at the store on the day before Thanksgiving and returned home suddenly. Now, after she's back at home, I get this awful feeling that the others are in danger. But it doesn't make sense: Mom would never do anything to harm Ella and Betsey.

Would she?

I fly through stoplights and make it to my street in the blink of an eye. At the gate, I pause before driving through, wondering if someone's inside the house. Sean calls again, but I let it go through to voice mail; I need to think. I can see Mom's car parked at the bottom; there are no other cars. I'm intensely afraid, but for Bet and Ella, I have to get over it.

I drive down, park, and run in.

"Hello?" I call from the entryway. "Betsey? Ella?" I wait a beat. "Mom?"

There's no answer. I call again. Still nothing.

I run from room to room on the main floor, searching for my family. Then I sprint upstairs and look in the rec room; the spy phone that I left for them is on the coffee table. Frantically, I check all four bedrooms and three bathrooms. I end up back in the entryway, turning around, directionless.

My cell rings.

"They're not here," I say. "Something's wrong. I can feel it."

"Maybe they just went out somewhere," Sean says. "Like after your mom came back. Maybe they went to find you."

"They didn't," I say. "I know it. They didn't call me

back and the phone is here; they wouldn't leave without it. I just know something's wrong."

"Because you can feel it," Sean says, almost a question.

"Yes," I say, a little snappily. "I can *feel* it. It doesn't happen all the time, but every once in a while, something happens, and the others know. I knew before Mom told me that Ella broke her arm when we were younger. Last month when I got home, Betsey was singing a song I'd been listening to in the car. It's like a form of telepathy. So yeah, I can feel it."

Instead of snapping back or telling me to calm down, Sean lowers his voice.

"Do you need my help?"

I think for a moment, then answer. "Yeah, I do. Meet me at my mom's office. I'll text you the address. I have an idea."

Sean's already at the office when I arrive, leaning against his car in the parking lot. He follows me inside the building, pausing to inspect Betsey's, Ella's, and my walls from the doorway of Mom's office like I did when I first visited. I don't stop this time; I rush to the desk and start opening drawers.

"What are we looking for?" Sean asks when he recovers and peels his eyes away from my wall. He joins me behind the desk; he's standing and I'm sitting.

"My mom has a terrible memory," I say. "She always writes things down." I yank a drawer divider out of the top left drawer so I can see under it. "Passwords. We're looking for passwords."

"Got it," Sean says, pulling a handful of files from the bottom right drawer and beginning the search.

My anxiety level grows with each passing second. Every five minutes at most, I pause to either call home or the other phone, or check my voice mail even though the spy phone's ringer is on high and it's been right next to me this whole time. Fifty minutes into the process, I'm about to start crying out of frustration when Sean pulls a little box out of the bottom of the file drawer across from the desk. With me watching, he opens it, then smiles.

"Bingo," he says.

"Oh, thank god," I say quickly, rushing over and grabbing the pink sticky note from his hands. It's just a handwritten list of strange number-letter combinations, with no explanation of which matches which account...she wouldn't make it that easy. But I breathe easier knowing that somewhere on this list is the key to finding Ella and Betsey.

I wake the computer, open the Internet, then start typing the name of a website that auto-fills thanks to Mom's frequent visits. I type my mother's email address into the username space, then start trying the passwords. At the very moment I hope that this isn't one of those sites that locks you out after too many failed attempts, I'm in.

"What is that?" Sean asks, peering at the map of the United States over my shoulder. There's a little green dot flashing on the screen, which gives me a small sense of relief.

Except that it's flashing over Nevada.

"It's them," I explain to Sean, touching my throat instinctively. "It's the necklace."

"Should we call the police?" Sean asks. "Report a kidnapping?"

"Except they don't exist," I mutter. "And besides, it's only been an hour. They'll never believe us." I pause for a few seconds. "Plus, we don't even know what happened."

"Lizzie, isn't it obvious that your mom...did something?" Sean says impatiently. "That she's behind this? I mean, look at this place." He gestures toward the walls. "She's been watching you three, and now, on the day you were going to expose her secrets, suddenly, she, Ella, and Betsey are gone. There's no way she isn't involved."

"Maybe," I say, unable to picture Mom forcing Ella and Betsey to go somewhere with her...without me. I shake off the thought.

"The only thing I can think to do is follow the tracker," I say, standing up from the desk with purpose. I start unplugging Mom's laptop to take with me, so I'll be able to see where they stop. If they're already in Nevada, they have to be on a plane. I stuff the computer, a power cord, and the Internet cable into a bag I find leaning against Mom's desk, then finally, I look up at Sean. He's watching me with an expression so serious my heart jumps. He doesn't have to say what he's thinking.

"You'll get in trouble," I protest without fire.

"I don't think I will," Sean says. "Once I explain everything, my mom will be okay. And besides, you're worth it."

"I don't know, Sean," I say. "I can't ask you to—"

"You're not asking," he interrupts, then takes a step toward me. He looks so determined, so strong. "I'm going."

Doing my best to think a few steps ahead, I take a couple of minutes to gather up some of the papers on Mom's desk and pull down a few notes from the boards. Maybe I'll need them as leverage; maybe I'm just wasting time. There's no way to tell now.

Sean follows me back to the house in his car; we both park in the driveway. We go inside, and hastily, I toss some clothes and my toothbrush into an overnight bag—I don't know how long this will take. When I'm ready to go, Sean convinces me to leave the sedan at home—his car is gassed up, and he's in a better frame of mind for driving. We stop by his house and he runs in and grabs some clothes, too; I stay outside and keep an eye out for his mom. Soon enough, we're on the freeway headed toward Los Angeles.

"This is definitely not how I thought this day would go," I say quietly, looking out the window as the tan landscape breezes by. I have my arms wrapped around my stomach because the nervousness is there: mine, and theirs, too.

"We'll find them," Sean says, resolute. "I promise."

I think that he shouldn't make promises that might be too big to keep, but I don't say anything. I appreciate the sentiment, at least.

"I'm just worried we'll be too late," I say. "They're moving really fast; they're obviously on a plane."

"We'll make it," Mr. Confidence says again. I smile at him, then realize something.

"But *how* are they on a plane?" I say aloud, not really asking Sean. Asking myself.

"What do you mean?" He glances at me, then back at the road.

"They don't have IDs," I say. "I mean, there's only one, and I have it. There's no way they could get on a plane without IDs."

"This guy my mom dated once was getting his pilot's license, and we went up with him," Sean says, blinkering to get around a pokey driver. "We just drove right out to the tarmac. It was a really small airport that did a lot of charter business. We didn't need IDs."

"They're on a *charter*?" I ask, thinking how beyond strange that seems, like we're in a James Bond movie or something. "Who charters airplanes anymore?"

Sean shrugs. "Rich people, I guess."

I think of Mom's mystery money and have to force myself to catch a breath. *What if she really did take them somewhere?*

"Can we listen to some music or something?" I ask, feeling like I might burst out of my skin I'm so anxious.

"Of course," Sean says, fishing his iPod out of the center console and handing it to me. "You pick."

I get us set with some road tunes, and eventually the music starts to make me feel better. Well, that, and Sean's hand resting on top of mine, sending me "calm" by osmosis.

We pull over outside of L.A. to check the tracker at a coffee shop that offers WiFi. The website is one of those that'll open only on the user's assigned computer and phone; it's frustrating that we have to stop every time I want to look—which happens to be frequently. Sean and I are jittery from all the coffees we're buying in order to use the Internet.

"It stopped," I say to Sean, pointing at the screen. He hands me a latte I don't want or need; I take a sip and set it aside.

"Where?" he asks, sliding into a seat on my side of the table.

"Denver," I say. "I wonder if that's the final destination." I stare at the blinking dot, willing it to give me the answer.

"Let's hope so," Sean says. He pulls his iPhone out of his pocket and starts tapping the screen; I lean over and see that he's looking at the GPS. I notice that his right knee is bouncing up and down; I push his latte aside, too. "We can make it there by morning if we drive all night."

"Sean," I say, looking at him, "that's crazy."

He laughs it off. "I'm good," he says. "I'm caffeinated, and running on ten hours of sleep and pure adrenaline. I'll stop if I get tired, but really, it's not a big deal."

I consider how badly I want to find Ella and Betsey, how much I need to make sure they're all right.

"Fine, but you have to let me drive part of the way."

"You got it."

twenty-six

I wake up the next morning in winter.

There's snow on the mountains and frost on the windows, and the road and landscape are the muted color of cold.

"You said you were going to wake me up!" I say, sitting up quickly and wincing at my stiff neck, then smacking Sean lightly on the arm. "Where are we, anyway?"

"Near Grand Junction, Colorado," Sean says before taking a sip of coffee from who knows where. "And I didn't wake you up because you needed some rest. But it was all good. I had my tunes and my thoughts to keep me company." He pauses, glances at me, then smiles. "You talk in your sleep."

"Oh, no," I groan, having heard it before. "What did I say?"

"Something that sounded straight from a Stephen King novel," he says, laughing. "You talked in this low monotone, like you were possessed. Don't worry, I couldn't understand what you were saying. But I gotta admit, it was late and dark and I might have screamed like a little girl . . . which didn't wake you, by the way."

"Sorry," I say, looking away, embarrassed but mostly amused. Then I remember that this road trip isn't about fun and silliness. "Let's pull over and check the tracker."

"I already did when I got coffee," Sean says. "They're actually not in Denver; they're in a town called Mystery. I Googled it; there's a college there. It's called Bramsford University."

"What the hell?" I ask, groggy and confused.

"I don't know, but we're only about four hours away. We'll find out soon enough." Sean looks at me and takes my hand. "Let's stop and eat, though, okay? I'm hungry, and you look like you could use some pancakes with whipped cream right about now."

"I couldn't do this without you," I say seriously. He squeezes my hand, but keeps his eyes on the road.

"Yes, you could," he says, "but I'm glad you don't have to."

When we're closing in on Mystery, Colorado, the tracker gives us a street address, which Sean punches into his car's

GPS. Happily, I retire the clunky laptop computer to the trunk. The closer we get to the town, the more insanely nervous I feel.

"Deep breaths," Sean says calmly. "We're going to find them."

"But what if we can't get to them?" I ask.

"We will."

I think that his confidence is borderline naïve, but it does help me mellow out a little bit. Soon enough, we're exiting the highway and pulling into Mystery.

Sean follows the GPS directions, turning right onto what I can tell is the university campus even though there are very few students around—it is Thanksgiving, after all. I see a sprawling, frost-covered lawn with crisscrossed walkways connecting old brick three-story buildings that look like they're part of a collection. Sean navigates around the U-shaped drive and ends up in front of a building marked Ashby Hall. According to the GPS, this is our destination. Sean pulls into a space marked VISITOR while a fresh onslaught of overzealous butterflies ravages my insides.

"They're in this dorm?" I ask, so confused my brain might explode.

"Is there any way your mom just took them on a college tour or something?" Sean says, grasping.

"On Thanksgiving?" I ask, laughing a short, high-pitched laugh like someone on the edge of crazy might. "Without me?"

"I know, it's a lame idea," he says, blowing on his hands.

Like the last survivors on an alien planet, a group of students huddled together walks by the front of the car. They're so bundled in beanie hats and big coats, you can barely see their faces. I shiver just thinking of getting out; Sean touches the dial on the heat again, but it's already up all the way.

"It's freaking frigid," Sean says. "We need coats."

"But we're here," I say, gesturing to the building.

"Yeah, but we're going to stick out like a sore thumb. I'm going out on a limb here, but I'm pretty sure Ella and Betsey aren't just waiting to greet us in the lobby. We're going to have to look around a little. We need to seem like we belong here."

I glance down at my light cardigan. And my flats with no socks.

"What if they go somewhere else by the time we get back?" I ask.

"Then we'll track them again," Sean says, smiling warmly. "Lizzie, it's taken us an entire night to get here; what's another half hour?" When he sees my face, he sighs. "How about if I run in and take a quick look around the lobby—just to make sure they really aren't sitting there, waiting for us?"

"Will you?" I ask.

In response, Sean pulls his hood over his head and opens the door. The kind of cold I've never felt before rushes into the car and pricks my exposed skin. Sean slams the door and runs across the sidewalk to the entrance; he's inside less than two minutes.

"There's a guy behind a reception desk, but there's no one else in the lobby," he reports when he's back in the driver's seat. His cheeks are red from mere seconds spent in the cold. "The good news is that the guy didn't see me; the bad news is that there's a sign on the desk that says 'ID REQUIRED.'"

"How are we going to get in?" I ask.

"I have no idea," Sean says, "but we'll think of something. But first... coats. We need coats."

We drive into the main part of town and stop at a discount store that happens to be open until noon. I toss a Bramsford University sweatshirt into the cart while Sean goes to find gloves. We both pick winter coats with hoods; mine has faux-fur lining. Sean pays using a credit card.

"Your mom is going to freak out," I say.

"No, she's not," he says. "I've talked to her twice, and she's okay."

"You have?" I ask. He nods.

"You were asleep," he says. Then, "I didn't tell her everything, but I told her a lot."

"And she's... okay with you just taking off?"

"Well, no, she's pissed, but she cares more that I'm safe," he says. "That *you're* safe, too." Sean looks at me seriously. "She wanted to call the police and let them handle it; I had to talk her out of it. But if we're not on the way back by tomorrow..."

"I get it," I say.

"And even then, we've got some explaining to do when we're back."

I think of Harper, and how she's the opposite of my mom. Harper is trusting, yet concerned; my mom is overbearing and self-absorbed. All Harper does is love and care for Sean, while, apparently, my mom is basically a stalker. And maybe a kidnapper, too.

Sean and I grab breakfast sandwiches from the food stand in the discount store, then get in the car and head back to Bramsford. We look like we fit in, but jealous of Sean's family, left alone by my own, I've never felt more like an outcast in my life.

twenty-seven

Sean and I park in the student lot next to the dorm this time around, thinking that emerging from the visitor section will only increase our likelihood of being stopped. It's a good idea except that the back window of Sean's car is very obviously missing a hot-pink student-parking sticker.

"They're not going to tow it on Thanksgiving," he says, locking the car. I try to burrow deeper into my hood, if that's possible; the wind here is arctic.

"You're mighty confident, you know that?"

He shrugs, then takes my gloved hand in his. "Remember the plans?"

"Plan A: You say that you lost your ID and hope the desk

guy is feeling charitable today," I say. "Plan B: We sneak attack up the back stairwell when he's not looking."

"That's right," he says, smiling like he's enjoying this. "And then we walk the halls, looking for your sisters."

Normally, the word *sisters* makes me cringe: It's a bitter reminder of my life in thirds. But not today. Today, it's real.

As it turns out, we don't need Plan A or Plan B.

"I didn't even notice that you left," the desk guy says as we approach. I turn and look behind me, thinking he's talking to someone else, but no one's there. His eyes are on me.

Oh!

"Yep," I say to the guy identified by his name tag as Jarrod. I smile warmly. "We went to get hot chocolate—"

"But it was closed," Sean cuts in when he sees Jarrod's confused expression.

"Right," I say, wondering if I should push it by saying I left my key in the room, hoping the room number would actually be printed on a replacement key. But Sean tugs on my arm before I can say more.

"Let's go up," he says. He shoots me a look like *Come on!* I take a step toward the elevators.

"Wait," Jarrod says from behind the desk. I freeze; my heart sinks. When I turn around, I try not to look busted.

"Yeah?"

"There's hot chocolate stocked in the lounge area on four," he says. "Just down the hall from your room."

"Thanks!" I say, feeling like I just won the car on a

246

game show or something. This guy thinks I'm either Ella or Betsey; he just told me they're on the fourth floor.

"Mugs are in the cabinet over the microwave," he calls as the elevator doors close. Too filled with fearful excitement, I don't answer.

The elevator doors open to a brick wall. I step out and look left and right but find nothing but a deserted hallway. It's just a dorm—and it's the middle of the day—but it gives me the creeps anyway. It smells like perfume and stale popcorn, with undertones of old. The wood floor living under the dingy blue carpet creaks when I step to the right. I walk about ten feet and peer around the corner at rows and rows of doors. All of which have decorated white boards on the outsides of them.

"Let's start on this side," I whisper to Sean; he nods and leads the way.

We creep down the hall to the first door. Scrawled at the top of the white board in cursive is *Welcome to the Home of Annie and Jamie.* I read, shake my head, and move on. The next board says *DINA AND CAITLYN* in bold caps. The one after that reads *Mandy's Room.* She must have a single.

Sean and I make it all the way to the end of the hallway. We turn the corner of the massive square and find the lounge that Jarrod the front desk guy mentioned. It connects the two hallways with a little living space that has a couch and two chairs, and a TV that looks older than my mom.

"Want some hot chocolate?" Sean whispers, clearly

trying to lighten the mood. I just roll my eyes and start across the room toward the other side.

Then I hear the elevator ding. I freeze, listening as a resident clomps down the hall we haven't checked yet, uses a key, and then lets the door slam behind her. At least I assume it's a *her*: All the doors we've seen so far have had female names on the boards. As far as I can tell, we're on a girls' floor.

When I'm sure the person's gone, I start down the hall, Sean following me this time, reading white board after white board. There are messages for the residents, phone numbers, and inspirational quotes, but I only care about the names at the top.

Ryanne and Serena

Teresa Territory

Whitney & Courtney

And then there it is: the blank white board. When I see it, I take a step back, like it's going to bite me. My heart feels like it's going to explode: I know they're inside. Whether they're alone or not is what concerns me.

I hear faint music, but it doesn't seem like it's coming from inside: It must be some other resident's room.

"Are you going to knock?" Sean whispers into my ear. I see movement under the door: not a lot, just a single shadow darkening the space between the carpet and the bottom of the door for a moment. Then it's gone.

"What if someone's in there with them?" I ask.

Sean pulls out his phone and dials 911. "I'll hit Call if anything happens," he says. "Want me to knock?"

"No, I'll do it," I say.

I move three steps toward the door, and then take a deep breath to try to calm my nerves. It doesn't help. I can feel the tension in every muscle in my body as I raise my hand and knock twice on the door. It's jarring in the quiet hallway. My heart leaps when I hear someone turn the door handle.

Then everything's okay.

"Betsey!" I say, rushing her and wrapping my arms so tightly around her torso that she makes a little oomph sound. She hugs back, and over her shoulder I see Ella stand up from the bed. She joins the embrace. When we part, I notice that they're both wearing warm jackets, like they were just about to leave.

Ella moves past me and peeks her head into the hallway. She looks left, then right, then steps back inside. "Get in here already," she says to Sean, waving impatiently. She closes the door, but not all the way.

"Did you see Mom on your way up?" she whispers.

"No," I say, shaking my head.

"Another woman? Blond?" she asks.

"No," I say. "No adults. The only person we saw was that guy at the front desk. Let's get out of here before we do see one of them." I want to ask so many questions—mostly about Mom's role in all of this—but I know that now's not the time.

"Okay, let's go," she says, grabbing her backpack from home and slinging it over her shoulder. Betsey does the same.

The four of us creep down the hallway toward the

elevator, but take the stairs instead. At the bottom, we see that the front desk guy is talking on the phone animatedly.

"He can't see us leave," Betsey says. "I have a weird feeling about that guy."

"I have an idea," Sean says. He looks at me excitedly. "Wait here—I'll be back." He turns and runs up the stairs; I hear a metal door open and close. Only because I'm staring into the lobby do I notice the doors on one of the elevators closing: It's been called to the third floor. Suddenly, the alarm goes off: The elevator is stuck. Just as I hear Sean coming back through the door and starting his descent, Jarrod the desk guy stands and wanders over to the elevator. He looks up at the numbers on the top and sees that it's stuck on the third floor. He glances at the stairwell, probably considering walking up, and we duck down below the little window. We wait a few seconds, then Betsey peeks.

"What's he doing?" Sean asks.

"Waiting for the other elevator," Bet reports. "You're a genius, Sean."

"I have my moments."

When Jarrod's safely inside the working elevator, the four of us tumble out of the stairwell, fly across the lobby, and rush into the blustery Colorado day. In minutes I'm leaving Bramsford University with Ella and Betsey next to me, and for the first time in twenty-four hours, I feel whole again.

twenty-eight

"Tell me what happened," I say the moment we're off campus. Betsey opens her mouth to respond, but then Sean turns in the opposite direction from the highway. "Where are you going?" I ask him.

"I'm going to try to rent a hotel room," he says. "I'm exhausted, and we need to figure out where we're going next. It seems like the smart thing to do."

"You can't rent a hotel room; you're not eighteen," Ella says.

"I've done it before on trips with my friends," Sean replies. "The eighteen thing isn't the law; it's policy. Sometimes they'll rent to you just as long as you have a credit card."

"And you do?" Ella asks.

"Yup."

We hold our conversation until we get to the hotel. Thankfully, Sean was right: He scores the room. We park near the back entrance, and the second I see the two double beds, I'm exhausted, too. But there's no way I can sleep.

"I think I'm going to take a shower," Sean says, pointing toward the bathroom. "That okay?" I'm sure he's curious about what's going on, but I love that he's respecting our need to talk about our family business in private. Not that I won't update him on everything later anyway.

"Fine with me," I say. Ella shrugs and Betsey smiles weakly. Sean takes his bag and closes the door; soon we hear the water running. I've loved having Sean with me on this trip, but when I find myself alone with Ella and Betsey, I'm relieved. Maybe it's because I don't have to put on a brave face anymore.

I sigh heavily as I plunk down onto the bed by the window. Ella sits on the same bed with her back against the headboard and her legs extended; Betsey joins us, folding her legs into a pretzel. I hug my knees and look from Betsey to Ella, then back again.

"So?" I ask when we're settled. "What the hell is going on?"

Ella's the one to talk; the usually boisterous Betsey is sedate.

"A while after you left, there was a knock at the front door," Ella begins. "I opened it, and it was this woman." She pauses, looking guilty. "I'd seen her before—I'd *talked* to her before... once at the bookstore. So when she asked to come in for a moment, I let her in. She said she had something important to tell me." Ella shakes her head at herself. "Who does that—who just lets a stranger in their house?"

"It's okay," Betsey says quietly. "You were caught off guard."

"How did she get to the front porch?" I ask, trying to sort out the logistics. "Through the gate?"

Ella shrugs. "Maybe she scaled it."

"My guess is that she walked through after you left," Betsey says, frowning. "We certainly didn't buzz her in."

"Anyway," Ella says, "she asked if anyone else was home, and that's when Betsey happened to come downstairs. Instead of acting surprised to see two of us, she said, 'Oh, good: the more the merrier.'"

"Who was she?" I ask, gripping my legs.

"Maggie Kendall," Ella says.

"Who's Maggie Kendall?" I ask.

"I'm getting to that," Ella says, crossing her legs and sitting up straighter, making herself a mirror of Bet's position. "There we were, standing in the entryway. She obviously wanted to come in, but I didn't invite her, so she just started talking. She didn't ask if Mom was home: I think she probably waited until she was gone to make her move.

"Maggie told us that she knew Mom in her old life— as a scientist. She said that she does the same type of genetic research that Mom used to do, and that she needed Mom's help."

"Why didn't she just ask Mom for Mom's help?" I say sarcastically.

"I guess she did, but Mom said no," Ella says. "Anyway, she pretty much told us that she wanted us to come with her to blackmail Mom. I mean, she didn't say it in those words, but basically. She said if we didn't come with her, she'd release Mom's name to the media and the FBI, along with photos of us."

"What?" I ask in disbelief.

"I'm serious," Ella says, and Bet nods. The water turns off in the bathroom, and I listen to the screech of shower curtain rings sliding along the rod.

"So you just *went*?"

"No judgment," Ella says sharply. "You have no idea what you would've done in that situation. And besides, she offered us something in return."

"What?" I ask, thinking that there's no way I'd have just left the house with a random stranger.

"Identities."

Apparently, what Maggie wanted was pretty reasonable, and what she was offering was a better life. Ella explains that Maggie's goal was to get Mom to spend a couple of weeks at her facility to try to fix a "hole" in Maggie's long-running research. All that was asked of Ella and Betsey was a plane ride, a long weekend in Colorado, and a few pints of blood and tissue samples. In return, Maggie would supply driver's licenses, birth certificates, and Social Security cards for them. There was no mention of me at all.

"But if she waited until I left to come through the gate, she had to have seen me," I say.

"Maybe she figured two was good enough," Betsey offers.

"Or maybe she thought that once she lured Mom to her, you'd follow."

I laugh bitterly. "I guess I did."

Sean emerges, and when I catch his eyes, he smiles at me so warmly that I want to go crawl into his arms. Instead, he casually walks across the room toward the door.

"I'll get us some food," he says quietly, not waiting for a response before leaving.

"It's nice he came with you," Betsey says.

"Yeah, it is," I say.

We're all quiet a moment before I ask when Mom showed up.

"Maggie called her," Ella says. "She told us to pack bags, then when we were ready, she called Mom and told her what was happening. She said, 'Come home quick, or your chickens will have flown the coop.'"

"That's when she ran out of the grocery store," I say, putting it together.

"I guess," Ella says. "Anyway, she came home in a hurry. They made us go in the other room; we heard them fighting for a few minutes, but then Mom just gave in. She came and got us and told us we were going to Colorado."

"Did she say anything about me?" I ask.

"She didn't," Ella says.

"She probably didn't think Maggie knew about you," Betsey says. "She was probably trying to keep you safe."

I frown at this, still wondering why Mom didn't call me. Then I remember that she had no idea where I was. That she'd taken our phone, and believed she'd also taken my secret cell, too. I'd left her no way of getting in touch with me.

"I felt your panic," I say quietly. "When did that happen?"

"When Mom and Maggie were arguing," Ella says. "Before then, I was sort of stunned, but then it all hit me and I completely freaked out. For a few minutes, when she just gave in so easily, I started to feel like Mom was somehow in on it. I whispered to Bet that we needed to get out."

"Which made me panic," Betsey says. "But there was no time; it was too late. They came and got us before we had the chance to act."

"Then you left with them?" I ask. "But Mom's car was in the driveway when I came looking for you."

"Yes, we went in Maggie's BMW," Ella says.

"Oh my god," I groan. "Is it red?"

"Yes," Ella says. "Why?"

"I've talked to her before, too," I say quietly. "At the gas station. And I've seen her car around. I wonder if I'd have said something . . ."

"There's no way you could've known," Betsey says.

"Seriously, no way," Ella echoes, but it doesn't make me feel better.

"Tell me about the plane ride," I say, wanting to change the subject.

Ella sighs. "Maggie and Mom made us sit in the back; they sat in the front, snapping at each other the whole ride. It was completely surreal." Ella rubs under her eyes and smears her mascara a little. "Then we landed and there was a car waiting to pick us up. It took us to the dorm.

"Mom went in with us, but she only stayed a minute—she went to Maggie's lab with her and stayed there all night. But before she left, she whispered into my ear, 'Where is Lizzie?'"

"What did you say?" I ask.

Ella shakes her head. "I didn't know what to say. I didn't know what had happened at the office, and if we had what we needed to confront her. So I just said that you went off with Sean." She looks sorry, like she's worried she got me in trouble.

"El, don't worry about it," I say. "We're way beyond me stressing about being grounded. And besides, Mom knows about Sean."

"What?" Betsey gasps.

"Totally," I say. "I'll tell you about it in a sec. But first, what else did Mom say to you before she left the dorm?"

Ella shifts. "She said she was going to leave you a message at home so you'd know we were okay. And then she said, 'Stay here—don't go out. I'll be back in the morning. You have to trust me that this will all be over soon. We'll go home and it'll be like this whole thing never happened.'"

"What did she mean by that?" I ask.

"Well, since she had no idea you were digging through her stuff, about to expose her," Ella says, "I think it meant that she thought we could just brush the whole hostage thing under the rug and go back to living as one person."

"Ugh!" I shout, blowing out my breath. "Why is she so . . . ugh!"

"I don't know," Ella says. "But that's when we decided that we most definitely weren't going to stay. The room didn't have a phone, so we couldn't call you, and we didn't want to leave at night—we had nowhere to go. The plan was to leave in the morning before Mom came back. But then you showed up."

We all look at one another with a lot of emotion behind our eyes, but no one says anything for a few moments. Then, finally, Bet says, "Now you tell us about the office."

Nodding, I begin the story of what happened after I left the house yesterday morning. I am all the way to the part about how Sean's call nearly scared me out of my skin when I realize that Sean's been gone for an awfully long time. I pause the conversation to text him.

WHERE ARE YOU?

PIZZA PLACE. OKAY TO COME BACK?

YES, AND BRING PEPPERONI!!!

I launch back into the story, and I'm too caught up in it to realize a few minutes later that it's only been a few minutes. There's a knock at the door, and I run over and fling it open. "Did you bring drinks or do we have to—"

"Hi, Lizzie," Mom says, frowning at me from the doorway. It hits me like a ton of bricks: the necklace. Of course Mom could find us as easily as I found Ella and Betsey. I want to smack myself on the forehead.

"May I come in?" she asks. She looks cold: Her nose is red and I can see her breath. I hate that I feel a twinge of sympathy; I hate that I step aside.

"I asked you to stay put," Mom says to Ella and Betsey. "You scared me."

"Where's the woman?" Betsey asks. "Maggie Kendall?"

"Out of our lives," Mom says flatly. "Don't worry about her again." She pauses. "Why didn't you stay in the dorms? Or leave a note?"

"Why did you want us to stay there, Mom?" Ella asks. "So we can go back to life as one person?"

Mom looks quizzically at her, probably sensing the mutiny in the room.

"I was just telling Ella and Bet what I found in your office, Mom," I say from behind her. "You know, the one with the stalker walls . . . one for each of us?"

As I walk by to join the others on the bed, I see Mom's mouth open a bit; she closes it quickly.

"We know you're not a doctor," Betsey says quietly.

"But that you still get money—and a lot of it—from *somewhere*," Ella says. "It's time to come clean. Tell us what's going on."

"So that's where you were?" she asks me. "Not with Sean?"

"That's where I was," I say, my eyes never leaving hers. "Looking at photos and weird notes about all three of us," I say, crossing my arms over my chest.

"It's how I keep track of my findings," Mom says quietly.

When she sees my horrified expression, she clarifies. "You three are my children, but you're also my job. When I took you from the clients all those years ago, it was maternal, yes—I wanted to protect you—but it was also a professional decision. The money you mentioned comes from a trust Dr. Jovovich set up to fund a lifetime of research. I am still and will probably forever be a geneticist."

"Were you ever a doctor?" Ella asks, letting the lies soak in. Mom shakes her head no, then pulls a chair from the table to the middle of the floor and sits down awkwardly.

"I want you to know that I care deeply for the three of you—I love you all," Mom says. "But I am also being paid to document your lives."

"Still?" I ask, focusing on facts instead of the fissure in my heart. "Dr. Jovovich is in jail."

"He is," Mom says, "but he set up the trust long before all that. I used to send him monthly reports on the three of you. The fact that he's in jail now makes this research even more important. Our agreement was to publish our manuscript when you turned eighteen—when you were through adolescence." She looks at me hard. "When you were adults."

"You're writing a *paper* on us?" I ask in disbelief.

"I'm writing the paper that will revolutionize science, Lizzie," Mom says, raising her chin a bit. "Everyone else is still cloning animals, too paralyzed by fear of the government to pursue human cloning. But we've succeeded. You're a success."

"Funny, I don't feel like much of one," I snap.

Just then Sean walks through the door carrying pizza. He stops, clearly shocked to see Mom. "Is everything okay?" he asks, looking at me and fishing for his cell phone. His distrust of her is obvious.

"It's fine," I say. "Come in. I'm starving." Then I look at my mother. "Besides, she was just leaving."

"Lizzie, let me explain. We need to talk about this, as a family." She glances at Sean.

I stand from the bed, then step closer to my mother and look her right in the eyes. In a measured tone, I say what needs saying: "We're not your family. That's the point. Please just leave us alone."

"Lizzie, I think you're being unreasonable," Mom says. "If you'd just—"

"I'm being unreasonable?" I shout, then compose myself before going on. "Mom, you forced us to live like one person for years, when, as far as I can tell, we didn't need to. You used us as guinea pigs in your little science project, lying to us the whole time. And god knows what you're going to say about two of us being *abducted*!"

"Lizzie, you're being dramatic," Mom says, holding up her hands. "Take a breath. What Maggie did was wrong, but she didn't exactly take them at gunpoint. And that's all over now; I solved the problem."

"I'm not dramatic!" I shout at her, disgusted that she'd help someone who kidnapped two of her children. "I'm awake! My eyes are finally open to this sham of a life you've created for us. I finally see how completely messed up it is . . . how messed up *you* are. You're positively delusional if you think I'm going to let you dictate one more minute of my life, do you understand?"

I stand up a straighter.

"*My* life, Mom," I say quietly. "Did you hear that part? I said *my* life."

"That's what we want," Betsey says from behind me. "We want our own lives back."

"And we're not taking no for an answer," Ella says.

I think of all of Mom's papers that I stole, of how I could blackmail her just like Maggie did. But in the end, I don't need to.

Knowing she's defeated—for now, at least—Mom stands and leaves the motel room. The four of us stare at one another in silence for a long time after she leaves. Then, Ella speaks.

"What just happened?" she asks.

"I don't know," I say, "but it's possible that from here on out, we're on our own."

Late that night, I'm wide-awake, watching Sean's sleeping body on the floor at the foot of Ella's bed. Betsey whispers something from the other side of the one we're sharing.

"What?" I whisper, turning over to face her.

"I said: It's either Mom or Maggie."

"What are you talking about?" I ask. "Are you asleep?" I sit up a little and squint into the darkness to see if her eyes are open. Eyes like mine stare back at me.

"If we want our own identities, we either have to make up with Mom or go back to Maggie," she explains. "Those are our two options, and both of them suck."

I think about this for a moment, then something hits me. "Maybe not," I say. "I might have a third option."

In the morning, when Betsey's showering, Sean's foraging, and Ella's drying her hair, I open Mom's laptop and log on. In thirty seconds, I confirm that, yes, I have a third option.

That is, if that option will cooperate.

twenty-nine

Four five-hour shifts later, we're in Northern California.

Nearing the end of the ride, Sean's at the wheel and we're listening to the kind of slow, heartstrings music that could put you to sleep if you weren't anxious about being minutes away from potential freedom. Well, hours.

"Tell me again why you think he's going to help us," Sean says quietly. I like that he uses the word us even though this isn't really his problem.

"He's helped us before," I say. "At least I think he did."

"What do you mean?"

"A guy helped us when we relocated—he got us the new ID for Elizabeth Best and helped Mom set up her corporation and stuff," I say slowly. "He works for the government or something, but he and my mom met in school. She never told us his name, but we used to call him the Wizard because he could conjure up identities out of thin air. Or at least he did that one time."

"And this is him? The guy we're going to see is the Wizard?"

I turn around to make sure Ella and Bet are still asleep. "I think so."

"You don't know for sure?" Sean asks, looking at me, surprised.

"He was the only person in my mom's address book that I didn't recognize."

"Are you being serious right now?" Sean asks quietly. "We've driven all this way to see someone who could be anyone?" He doesn't sound mad, just tired.

"Yeah, but when I saw his name, I just knew it was him." I look at Sean, and he glances at me, then back at the road. "I know it's him."

"I guess we'll find out soon," he says with a small smile. "But you have good instincts: I'm sure you're right. At least, I *hope* you are."

"I'm right," I say, hoping that I am, too. Then I yawn. "Hey, we have to stop somewhere until morning. It's the middle of the night; we can't show up now."

"Good call," Sean says, yawning too. Which makes me yawn again.

We start through a tunnel originating in Oakland and dumping us out in a town called Alameda. It looks cute, but it's dark and my eyes are fuzzy from trying to read using a convenience-store flashlight, so I'm withholding judgment until the morning. Sean finds us a hotel, where we sleep for not enough hours. Then by the light of the too-bright California sun, we pull into a driveway in front of a massive Victorian; we're filled with a lot of nervousness but also, though this part goes unspoken, high hopes.

The four of us get out and walk up the steps. The day assaults my sleepy eyes; I squint as I reach over and ring the bell. It's one of those doorbells you expect to be answered by a butler. Instead, a man about Mom's age opens the door. Not to be gross, but he's kind of hot.

"Hi," I say nervously, thinking maybe we should've called first like Bet suggested. I force myself to speak. "Are you Mr. Weller?"

"I am," the man says. The sun is right behind us; he's squinting at me sideways. "How can I help you?"

For a split second, I think we've driven all this way for nothing. That I'm standing in front of one of Mom's former coworkers or her high school sweetheart. But then a cloud blocks the sun and I see the look in his eyes: It's recognition. I was right.

"We're here to find out whether you can get us new identities," I say bluntly. I hear Ella suck in her breath a little; it's probably not how she'd have done it.

"That's quite a request," he says warmly. "Come on in and we can talk about it." He holds the door open, welcoming us into his home like we're long-lost relatives. His face is friendly, but I don't miss his deadpan glance down the street before he closes the door.

Who or what is he looking for?

"I'm Lizzie," I say as I step inside. "That's Ella and that's Betsey."

"And I'm the driver," Sean says, extending a hand.

"Sorry," I say, "I'm tired. That's my boyfriend, Sean." Sean laughs quietly when we catch glances.

"Nice to finally meet you all," the man says with a smile. He shuts the front door; it's cool and quiet inside the large house. "Your mom's an old friend; that makes us friends, too.

"Please . . . call me Mason."

After a lot of explaining on our part, we wait in the comfortable living room while Mason calls Mom from the kitchen. He says he wants to tell her we're all right, but I think he's also asking permission to help us.

"Your mother said to call her later," Mason says, returning from the kitchen with a bowl of pretzels in one hand and a tray of sodas in the other. "Here, I thought you might be hungry."

Sean wastes no time digging in, but Betsey, Ella, and I look at Mason expectantly.

"And?" I ask when I can't take it any longer.

"And it's fine," he says, half smiling. "I'll do it." He pauses, then stands up. "It'll take about a day, so you're welcome to stay here tonight. In fact, I insist that you do."

"Thank you," Ella and I say in unison. He laughs a little.

"Let's start with pictures—for your driver's licenses and passports."

Ella frowns. "Can I brush my hair and teeth first?" she asks. "I mean, I'll be carrying those things around *forever*." Mason nods.

"Of course," he says. "The bathroom's upstairs at the end of the hall. You girls can drop your bags in the green room or the disaster with the chalkboard paint." He looks at Sean. "You can bunk in the blue room."

I stop in the doorway of a room so cool I want to steal it and take it home with me. There's funky vintage furniture mixed with clean lines, and girls' clothes strewn here and there. I smile at the quotes chalked over the bed and the mismatched but harmonious posters on the walls. I notice more than a few photos of a guy who's not quite as hot as Sean but still double take–worthy. The room is organized chaos.

"I want to sleep in here," I say to Ella when she walks up behind me.

"Be my guest," she says. "I'll take the nice, neat guest room across the hall over this any day, even if I have to share the bed with Betsey. Who could live in here?"

"Me," I say quietly, but Ella's already moved on.

I go in and drop my bag on a floral chair, then take a closer look at the photos on the massive corkboard. It's easy to tell which smiling face is the owner of this room: Pretty, with enviable blond hair and really light blue eyes, she's the common denominator in the pictures. There she is with the cute guy; there she is with a bunch of girls at an amusement park, caught mid laugh. There she is with a girl with super cool two-toned blond-and-black hair. My eyes linger on the other girl's hair for a moment, and suddenly, inspiration strikes.

"You guys!" I shout, rushing out of the room and across the hall to the guest bedroom.

"What's up?" Ella says, turning to face me. She's got her toothbrush sticking out of her mouth, so it sounds like *wus-ah*.

"Yeah, where's the fire?" Betsey asks. She seems more herself now that we're far away from Colorado, and far away from Mom.

"I have the best idea ever," I say confidently. "We just need to stall Mason for a few hours. And find a drugstore, stat."

After we attack the beauty aisle of the local drugstore and the teen section of the discount clothing store, Sean and I hang back at a coffee shop while Betsey and Ella check one more place. We're just sitting down at a table when his cell rings; he frowns and answers it. I listen to his side of the conversation; when he hangs up, he doesn't look happy.

"My mom wants me to come home," he says.

"Today?" I ask, feeling my heart sink.

"Yeah," he says. "She's been cool up to this point, but now that you're safe..."

"I get it," I say. "I'm surprised she didn't make you turn around and come home two days ago."

"She knew you needed me, and she trusts me," he

says. "But I missed Thanksgiving and...you know. Moms."
I don't really know, but I don't say that.

"You should drop us off at Mason's and get on the road," I say, every part of me wanting to inhale those words back into my mouth.

"How will you get home?" he asks. I consider it for a moment.

"I guess we'll fly," I say. "We'll have to get our mom to buy the tickets, but I'm sure she'll have no problem doing that if it means we're coming back to San Diego." I take a sip of my latte. "I mean, we'll have our own IDs; we might as well test them out."

My stomach flips over at the thought.

Sean and I don't make a big thing of saying goodbye—everyone is watching—but I feel the tug of him when his car rounds the corner and disappears. I can't help it: I text him.

I'LL SEE YOU IN THREE DAYS, TOPS.

He writes back,

HOPING 4 2

Knowing he's driving, I don't respond.

A few hours later, an unruffled Mason takes our pictures, calls Mom about the plane tickets, and leaves us in the living room with the remote and a free pass to eat anything in the fridge while he goes to work on the business of fabricating our identities. Ella, Betsey, and I don't talk much that afternoon or evening—we just sit together, show-hopping and being. We go to bed early, and in the morning, we pack up and wait for the cab that Mason prepaid to take us to the Oakland airport.

In the entryway, Mason hands each of us a yellow envelope with a clasp on the top. I peer into mine and find my new driver's license, passport, birth certificate, transcripts, medical history, and Social Security card. Like a true wizard, Mason basically just handed me a new life.

"Thank you," I say, looking at him sincerely.

"You're welcome," he says. "And don't forget to hold on to my number."

"We won't," I say.

Ella echoes my thank-you, but Betsey actually hugs Mason, which seems to surprise but not repel him. He half smiles when he realizes what's happening, then hugs her back. The others step onto the porch when the cab pulls up, but I claim to have forgotten something upstairs. I run up to the girl's room and grab the chalk from a tray on her nightstand. In small print near the edge of the space, I write a short note.

I love your room. Hope to meet you someday.—Lizzie Best

I'm not sure why, but I feel a connection with the girl. Maybe it's as simple as liking her stuff and wanting to make a new friend now that I can. Or maybe it's the fact that we both have totally weird parents: We're the same, in a way.

I join the others in the cab, and in less than twenty minutes, we're standing in the airport security line. It moves quicker than I'm ready for, but when the agent checks my ID against my boarding pass, then glances at my face, all he does is stamp the document and hand everything back to me.

Mom's waiting for us at baggage claim. I hold my chin high as we approach, hyperaware of what we look like and Mom's face as she notices the differences.

Betsey's long dress flows behind her in the breeze from moving, as does her newly dyed fire-red mane. Ella is preppy chic in a cardigan with a cute collar underneath, skinnies, and flats; the way Bet cut Ella's naturally curly bob shows off her defined cheekbones. As for me, I walk tall in a short skirt, a black long-sleeved T-shirt, and lace-up boots with thick, patterned tights. Bet really showed off her hairstyling skills when she chemically stick-straightened my hair, then made it perfect with a royal-blue stripe down the front.

We walk across the expanse, feeling as different on the outsides as we are on the insides. I can see in Mom's eyes that she gets it: That she finally *sees* us. I can see in her eyes that she knows we'll never be the same. That she knows that no matter how much she may want to try to brush things under the rug and make us live like we were, no amount of coaxing or forcing will help.

Permanent dye is our insurance policy.

thirty

Though it feels like we've been gone months, we return to our house on the hill five days after we left it. We've missed no school; everyone's still on Thanksgiving break. Nothing has changed, and yet, to me, the world is in color for the first time. I keep checking my driver's license to make sure it's real.

I text Sean as Mom pulls the car through the gate:

WE'RE BACK

He responds:

WHEN CAN I SEE YOU?

Smiling, I glance up at my mom in the mirror, at her determined face.

SHE WANTS TO TALK TO US. NOT SURE HOW THIS IS GOING TO GO. WILL CALL YOU AFTER.

Sean texts back:

GOOD LUCK.

"Go drop your stuff in your rooms and meet me in the living room," Mom says when we're all inside. "I think it's time the four of us had a good, long chat."

Ella, Betsey, and I do as she says. Upstairs, my room looks too boring, too bland. I wish I could go to the mall and buy some more posters, but instead, I have a tongue-lashing to look forward to. I head back downstairs, bracing myself for trouble. But when I step into the living room, there's a pint of ice cream on the coffee table—not even on a coaster—and bowls and spoons stacked to the side.

"I thought mint chip might make things easier," Mom says, smiling weakly. I think of all she's done, and I can't smile back.

But I do accept the ice cream.

"First, I want to say how sorry I am for what happened this weekend," Mom says, brushing her hair out of her eyes.

"What did happen?" Ella asks. "I'm still...I don't really know why that woman did what she did."

Mom sighs. "Maggie Kendall's team tried to do what ours did: They tried to clone humans," Mom says. "They were unsuccessful, or so I thought."

"What does that mean?" Betsey asks.

"I'll get to that in a minute," Mom says. "Anyway, they played dirty, luring lab assistants to their space and trying to get them to share secrets. They tried to recruit me, and I'll always regret taking the interview. For a while now, I've believed that Maggie was the one who turned in Dr. Jovovich. She's a big part of the reason I've been looking over my shoulder all these years."

I reach back and yank a throw pillow out from under me and toss it aside. I want to ask why Maggie just suddenly turned up now, but I don't want to speak to Mom. Honestly, I'm not sure I trust a word she's saying anyway.

Like she heard my thoughts, Ella asks, "How did Maggie find us?"

Mom looks away quickly, then back at Ella. Then her eyes fall on mine. "Lizzie, this isn't your fault," she says in a way that makes me think she's saying it is my fault. "But she found us through Twinner...when you uploaded the photo of yourself and got a match." She looks at Betsey when she says the next part. "I said earlier that I thought that Maggie hadn't been successful cloning humans; I was wrong. Her team had been monitoring Petra."

"Oh my god, she is the Original?" Betsey says excitedly.

"No, no," Mom says, raising her palms. "Maggie said that when Dr. Jovovich and I claimed to have failed with the cloning, the clients went to her team next. They apparently succeeded one time, but the DNA wasn't right. Apparently, she has something similar to progeria, but not nearly as severe."

"What's that?" Betsey asks, concerned.

"It's when you age too quickly," Ella says.

"Good," Mom says to El, like we're in class instead of talking about the fourth human clone. "That's right. It's rapid aging, and usually children with that issue have a life expectancy of only twenty years, tops. But in this case, it's a mutation of that disease that's much slower progressing. But still . . ." Her words trail off.

"Petra's going to die?" Betsey asks. Mom doesn't answer at first. Then, "I'm sorry, but yes, in her thirties or forties," she says. "I know you've emailed with her. I know—"

"What don't you know?" I mutter under my breath. It just flies out of my mouth; I didn't mean to speak.

"Not a lot," Mom says. She sounds more worn-out than proud. I look down at my forgotten bowl of ice cream; it's a green-and-brown soupy mess.

"How did Petra end up in Oregon?" Bet asks.

"Apparently, the clients didn't want to risk having another baby die on them, so they put her up for adoption."

"That's . . ." Betsey says, her words trailing off.

"Yes." Mom shifts in her chair.

"So where's Maggie?" Ella asks. "What's to stop her from coming back here and trying again?"

"Blackmail," Mom says flatly. "I have a little recorder in my car that I turned on when I came home that day. You might remember Maggie from TV back when Dr. Jovovich went to jail. She was quoted on the news saying human cloning is unethical and those who were secretly doing it deserved to be punished. Little did they know, she was one of those people."

Mom takes a breath; I realize I'm holding mine.

"Anyway, she's kept up that front, and I recorded her saying that she cloned Petra." She pauses. "That morning you took off, I went to her and played her the recording. I told her never to come near us again or she'd go to jail like Dr. Jovovich."

Mom waits a moment, maybe hoping one of us will ask about her fate—about Maggie turning Mom in right back. When we don't, she fills in the blanks.

"If she tries to turn me in, she'll fail. I have triplets—each with her own Social Security card and identity."

Suddenly, the license in my purse feels less shiny, because it seems like it was Mom's idea, not mine.

"You didn't know we were going to ask Mason for help when you talked to Maggie," Betsey says. She looks confused.

"I didn't," Mom says. "At that moment, I wasn't thinking of myself. I was thinking of you."

I can't help it: I roll my eyes. She sees me but doesn't say anything. At this point, I'm not sure what she could say.

"Wait a minute," Ella says, working something out. "If you had a recorder, why didn't you just end it right after she told you she cloned Petra? Why did you go along with her? Why did you allow us to go along with her?"

Mom blushes. "It wasn't the best choice I've ever made."

I furrow my eyebrows at her. "What do you mean?" Choice?

"I assessed the situation and didn't feel like any of us were in life-threatening danger, so..." Mom stops talking just as it hits me. Suddenly, I know why she let us panic, let two of us think we were being kidnapped and the other one go on a wild-goose chase across the country in winter weather.

"She wanted to see Maggie's lab," I say disgustedly. "She wanted to see her research."

The way my mom purses her lips together tells me two things. First, I'm right. And second, no matter what she says, science comes first.

"I'm done talking," I say, standing up and leaving the living room. Over my shoulder, without looking back, I say it again. "I'm done."

No one else comes upstairs for a long time. I call Sean and tell him about everything; we talk for a few minutes, but then he has to go because his mom is instituting Quality Family Time after he missed her favorite holiday.

"I could get out of it," he says, "if you want to come over. Or I'll come there? I mean, now that she knows about us..."

"She always knew about us," I say, which makes me feel a little sick. Then, "I don't feel like I can leave right now. They're still talking down there; I want the update from Bet and Ella later."

"But you don't want to go down and hear it yourself?"

"I can't," I say. "I don't want to be near her."

"I get it," Sean says. "Are you sure you don't want me to ditch my mom? We can talk on the phone all afternoon."

"Thanks, but go spend some time with Harper," I say. "You're lucky to have her for a mom. And I'm fine." I sigh, looking around. "I think I'm going to rearrange my room."

Later, when the bed's on the opposite wall and I've taped my photos into a funky swirl pattern over the headboard, there's a soft knock at the door. Ella peeks in; Betsey pushes her way through.

"That's really cool," Bet says, pointing at the pictures before flopping down next to me.

"Mom left," Ella says, joining us. I don't ask where she went.

"So?" I ask, staring at the ceiling. "What else did she say?"

"She did a lot of apologizing," Ella says. I shake my head. *Of course she did.*

"She told us all about her research... basically the

279

same stuff she said in Colorado, but with some extremely nerdy moments between her and this one over here," Betsey says, hooking a thumb at Ella.

"But the biggest thing we talked about was how it's going to work now," Ella says, rolling onto her side to face me.

"Tell me," I say nervously. "Can't wait to hear what scheme Mom's come up with this time."

"It's not a scheme, actually," Ella says. "She's letting us pick where we go to school."

"What?" I ask, surprised.

Ella nods. "She said we're going to go back to living as triplets."

It's what I knew was coming—it's what this blue stripe in my hair helped ensure—but it feels like a lackluster victory. It feels like doing philanthropy for school credit—like someone forced you to do it.

We forced her.

"Only one of us can go back to Woodbury, and we all know who that's going to be," Betsey says, smiling at me. I think of school with Sean and can't help but smile back. "Mom said El and I can choose different schools and she'll have Mason do his best to get us in midyear."

"That's great," I say, unable to make the tone in my voice anything but just . . . there.

"What's wrong?" Bet asks, tipping her head to the side. "These are good things."

"Don't you guys see that Mom's just trying to bribe us

into being okay with everything?" I ask, annoyed that they're being so naïve.

"Of *course* we get it," Ella says, looking at me seriously. "If nothing else, this whole experience has let us see Mom's true colors. But hey, if her guilt about screwing up our lives thus far gets me a seat in a classroom at a private school far away from David Chancellor, I'm all for it."

"I look at it like my ticket to a totally new experience," Betsey says earnestly. "I want old brick buildings and even older professors and...fall. I want to move to New England."

Ella sucks in her breath as my head snaps in Betsey's direction.

Bet smiles; she looks so lovely with her bright red hair. "Will you guys kill me if I ask to go to boarding school?"

Late that night, I wander into the kitchen in search of water; Mom's sitting at the table when I turn on the lights. I gasp loudly.

"You scared me!" I say.

She laughs a little. "Sorry," she says, "I couldn't sleep. I was just thinking." I don't ask about what.

I move to the cabinet and get a glass, fill it, and chug my water. I put the glass in the dishwasher and turn to leave.

"Lizzie, come sit down a second," she says.

I don't want to, but I do it anyway.

"I'm sorry that I lied to you," she says. It disarms me.

"It's not okay," I say quietly. "I don't forgive you." Then, "Mom, I know that you're trying to make things right. I appreciate that you let Mason give us our identities, and that we can pick our schools. But..."

"You need time," she says. "I know."

"I'm not sure time will fix it," I admit. "I really just..." I look her right in the eyes. "I don't trust you anymore."

She flinches, just a little, but enough.

"You have every right not to," she says sadly. "But I'm going to keep trying to make it up to you. And in the meantime, can we have a truce?" Her voice catches and she coughs. "Can we be more open with each other?"

"I guess," I say.

"All right," Mom says. "It's a start." She stands up from the table and takes a step toward the door, but not before smoothing down my hair. I want to pull away, but I don't; as much as I hate so many things she's done, I don't hate the affection.

"The hair," she says. "I like it."

I turn in my chair and look at her; she has tears in her eyes but she sniffs them away. "The blue suits you."

After she's gone, when I walk through the entryway and catch a glimpse of myself, I take comfort in knowing that she was right about something, at least. And as she said, it's a start.

thirty-one

My part is no longer first half.

Student government, chemistry, trigonometry, psychology, Spanish, dance, and creative writing are all mine to love or loathe, to pass or fail.

"Ready for this?" Sean asks the morning of my first day back. We're in the student lot; we drove together in Sean's car. It's crisp and bright outside, and I'm wearing an outfit that I picked out by myself. My hair is sleek, and despite my nervousness, I'm smiling.

"I think so," I say, grabbing Sean's hand. As we make our way toward the school, we get a lot of attention from other kids. Maybe it's because we're still a new couple; maybe it's because of my makeover. Most likely, it's a bit of both. Little do they know that what's changed is so much more than my hair.

When our reflections show up on the outside of the glass near the doors, Sean says quietly, "You know you look ridiculously hot, right?" My stomach flips; I squeeze his hand.

"I adore you," I say, "and not just for the compliments."

Dave looks surprised by my appearance in student government, but he otherwise leaves me alone, which is just fine by me. Chemistry and trigonometry are less nightmarish than I expected; between trig and psych, I run into Alison in the hallway.

"Elizabeth, your hair is awesome!" she says, smiling brightly.

"Thanks!" I say back. "Did you have a good Thanksgiving?"

"Ugh, the usual," she says, shrugging. "Turkey, family drama, forced board games. How about you?"

"It was pretty uneventful," I say. "Hey, let's get coffee again sometime soon."

"Anytime!" Alison says, her face brightening.

"How about today?" I ask. She looks surprised.

"What about cheer?" she asks. "Don't you have practice?"

"I'm quitting," I say, trying to look disappointed. "I pulled a muscle in my calf that won't heal if I keep cheering. Plus my mom's making me get a tutor. Apparently I suck at science."

"Not as much as I do!" she says, laughing. "Well, I'm sorry about your leg—and the tutor—but I'm glad you'll have more time to hang out. Meet you after school by your locker?"

"It's a plan." I turn to go, then look back. "Hey, Alison?"

She looks at me expectantly. "Yeah?"

"My friends call me Lizzie," I say. "I hope you will, too."

When I get home from school, Ella and Mom are in the living room together. I catch a snippet of the conversation: Ella's talking about her new school.

"...just so much more challenging, in a good way," she says.

"You've always been my overachiever," Mom says, smiling warmly.

"I take that as a compliment," Ella says, smiling back.

Then they notice me standing there.

"Lizzie!" Mom says, sitting up straighter in her chair. "Come join us. Tell us how your first day back went."

The scene is so normal—just a mom and a daughter bonding. I could try to bond, too. But something keeps me frozen in the doorway, something that smells a lot like distrust. It's self-centered, but in a way I feel like Mom wronged me most. Maybe it's that I found her out; maybe it's because she wouldn't let me date Sean. Maybe it's because she's still never apologized for just *leaving* me in San Diego when Maggie came knocking.

"It was fine," I say, hiding my emotions. The day was

a lot more than fine, but I'm not ready. Mom and I may have a truce, but that doesn't mean I have to overshare. "I'm getting a soda and going up to do my homework. Sean's coming over later."

I stare at Mom, waiting for her to protest. Waiting for her to say that Sean's not good for my image, not good for me. Waiting for her to Mom me.

Instead, she says, "He seems like a nice boy." And then, "There's soda in the garage; bring in a bunch, will you?"

"Happy New You," Sean says, beaming, when I open the front door. I check out his un-gelled hair, thermal shirt, black hoodie, faded jeans, and sneakers and think that he's my brand of perfect. He's holding out a wrapped present; I take it and smile curiously.

"You're so sweet," I say. "What is it?"

"You'll have to wait and see."

"Get in here," I say, grabbing him by the shirt and pulling him across the threshold. "Want to go out back?"

"Sure," he says, reaching out and touching my hair. "Anywhere is fine."

Sean follows me through the kitchen and into the living room, where I grab a blanket off the back of the couch. We go out the double doors to the back patio. Without me asking him to, Sean pushes one of the lounge chairs right next to the other; we sit and I drape the blanket over both of us.

"Okay," he says when we're settled. "Open it."

I rip the paper before the words are fully out of his mouth. Sean laughs while I eagerly pry open the box. I suck in my breath when I see the silver bracelet with a heart locket.

"There's a picture in there," he says, pointing to the charm.

Thankful that the porch sensor lights are still on, I pop it open and feel a rush of emotion when I see the tiny framed photo of me and Sean at his mom's studio that day so long ago. He's standing behind me with his arm around the top of my shoulder and across my chest like he's protecting me. Our faces are pressed together. Sean's looking at the camera and his mouth is near my ear; my face is dipped down and to the right like I'm listening to him tell me a secret.

"I wonder what you were saying to me in this picture."

"I know what I was thinking," he says.

"What's that?"

"That I love you."

A breeze picks up and I shiver, but not because of the weather. I look into Sean's eyes and feel like I'm going to burst. I owe him so much, for his friendship and support, for his love and honesty. For seeing the real me before the rest of the world had the chance to.

"I love you, too," I say, and then I kiss him, just as the motion-sensor lights click off.

thirty-two

One month later, the day after Christmas, Mom lets Ella and me take Betsey to the airport alone. I know Mom wants to come, but I also know that she's done controlling us for now. I can only hope that it's because she's trying to give back some of the freedom she stole away.

Instead of hugging goodbye at the curb, Ella parks and we walk Betsey inside. We've never left one another before, and Ella and I prolong it by getting into the security line with Bet and snaking around as far as we can go.

"Promise not to come back next summer with a Massachusetts accent?" I say, rounding a corner and stepping to the left to avoid someone's suitcase.

"Why?" Betsey says, laughing. "They're wicked awesome."

"We'll text every day, okay?" Ella says, making a pinkie promise without the childish gesture. Betsey nods.

"We will," I agree. We're almost to the front of the line.

"You know," Betsey says, glancing at the two people ahead of her. She takes a few steps forward and we follow. "We haven't said it in years, but you guys *are* my sisters. But more than that, you're my best friends." She looks from Ella to me. "Don't forget that, okay?"

"I won't," I say, unable to hold back the tears. It makes Ella and Bet cry, too; we all hug, then wipe tears on our shirtsleeves and sniff back runny noses.

"Driver's license and boarding pass," the security agent says with no emotion, despite our blubbering. Bet sniffs one final time and gets it together; this calms Ella and me. Betsey hands the items to the guy, then looks at me and says quietly, "It's okay to forgive her."

There's no time to answer; the man waves her through. But I'm not sure I would've said anything if there were.

Ella and I hop out of line and watch Bet take off her shoes and jacket and go through the metal detector. When she's on the other side, she stops, turns, and holds up a hand. A hand that matches mine.

"Live your life," I whisper to her. There's no way she hears, but somehow I know that she understands. She nods at me, then walks away.

"Come on, let's go," I hear from behind me.

I turn to see Ella moving toward the exit to the parking lot, expecting me to follow. I look from her to Bet and back again, watching them pull away from me in different directions, marveling at how whole I feel in spite of it. I've craved individuality, but a little part of me feared that with it might come loneliness, too. But I don't feel lonely today; I feel full. I feel strong.

Smiling, I look once more at my sisters—left, then right.

Ella is on one path. Bet's on another.

And I'm okay right where I am.

epilogue

Two weeks before our eighteenth birthday, Mom gives Ella and me early presents: plane tickets to visit Betsey in Massachusetts so we can celebrate the milestone together. To save on parking costs, Mom drops us at the airport with a typical "goodbye and be careful." We enjoy the Birthday of a Lifetime that weekend, but when Ella and I return, we find Sean waiting to pick us up.

"I'm so glad to see you!" I say, hugging him hard.

"It was your mom's idea," he says before kissing me on the forehead.

"How nice of her," I say without feeling. We're fine, Mom and I, but that's all we are. A year ago, I thought I'd move past everything that happened eventually, but somehow, it manages to stick with me. "Let's go," I say to Sean, not wanting to talk about my mom. "I have about five million pictures to show you."

Somehow Mom makes the day about her anyway.

Her car isn't out front, and when we walk into the house, I feel it immediately. There's something about the stillness. And it's stale, like no doors have been opened in a while. My stomach clenches, and in the periphery, I see Ella put her hand on her belly. The phone rings; it's Bet.

"What's wrong?"

"I'm not sure, but I think..." I begin, looking at Ella. She nods. "I think so, too."

"Bet, she's gone," I say into the phone. "Mom's gone."

To my beautiful daughters—

Eighteen years and nine months ago, I made the best decision of my life. It gave me purpose: It gave me you. Since then, I've made some bad choices, and there's only one way to make things right.

I'm turning myself in to the FBI.

I used to live in fear that someone would expose you as clones. After Maggie, I realized something: They are fascinated by you, but they need me. You are someone else's successes; they want their own.

I didn't blackmail Maggie in Colorado—I didn't have a recorder. I went along with her not out of curiosity but out of fear. I'm so sorry I couldn't reach you, Lizzie. I know you must have been terrified.

Ultimately, I made a deal with Maggie that I would help with her research…but not until you three turned eighteen. I wanted to make sure that if anything happened to me, you'd be safe from the system. But I had no intention of helping her. I needed to finish my paper and publish, then turn myself in before she had the chance. That would take away her leverage.

(Just in case, I paid one of Maggie's research assistants to steal a few incriminating files that would surely send her to prison. Maggie is much too interested in self-preservation to bother you again, but if someone else ever did, you have your ironclad identities to refute their claims.)

I've attached my manuscript titled "The Originals: Raising Clones Together, as Individuals." In it, I generally share the formula for creating human clones, but it's nothing that science doesn't know already. I chronicle the development of three female clones until their eventual deaths at the ages of six, eight, and nine. This is the only thing that is untrue in the study, but I wanted you to be protected.

No one will know you exist.

The paper will be published in next month's Science journal, and will be attributed to me, Sonya Bauer, and Dr. Allen Jovovich. The name "Best" will never be mentioned.

Mason is available for assistance, and please contact me only through him, for your safety. I am confident that there

will be a day when we'll be reunited. Until then, please know
that I love you more than anything. More than living. And
though some of you may still not believe this, I love you more
than science.

Mom

Five months later, I proudly walk across the Woodbury stage wearing a cap and gown to accept my diploma. Sean's mom and Betsey clap for me from the front row, and I'm not sure, but I'll bet Mason's watching from the shadows, where I'm realizing he prefers to be. Sean's beaming from the K section, waiting his turn. Bet graduated last week; we'll race to Ella's ceremony after this.

"Is that your sister?" Alison asks after it's all over, pointing. I smile at the furious waver on the other side of the sea of people. "Yep," I say proudly. "That's Bet."

"I love her hair," Alison says. "Oh my god, I hope she likes me. I mean, sharing a quad with three sisters is going to be—"

"Awesome," I say, side-squeezing her. "Everything about Berkeley is going to be amazing."

Especially since Sean will be there, too.

I rush through the crowd and get crushed by hugs the second I reach Harper, Betsey, and Sean.

"Come on, you guys, we need to go!" I say.

"You need your moment, too, honey," Harper says. "This is your moment." I love how much she's stepped up since Mom left; she and Mason are like weird, unmarried surrogate parents. She's in charge of making sure I'm fed, while he's in charge of doling out funds from the trust Mom set up, and looking protectively over my shoulder.

Harper tells Sean and me to hold still for a picture, and I know from the way she smiles at the screen afterward that it's going to be a framer. Finally, I get everyone to move it already; we walk to Harper's car, Sean and me swinging our clasped hands.

"Congratulations," he says, kissing my knuckles.

"Same to you, graduate," I say, nudging him.

We're almost to the car when, out of nowhere, Mason appears.

"Hello, Lizzie," he says. "Congratulations."

"Thank you," I say. "Thanks for coming."

"I'm happy to be here," he says, pulling something from his pocket. "But also, I wanted to give you this." He holds out a small box; my stomach flips, because I'm pretty sure I know who it's from.

"Mom?" I ask quietly. He nods once before patting me on the shoulder and turning and walking away.

"That guy's so weird," Sean says when Mason's out of earshot.

"Yeah," I say, "but he's pretty great, too."

In the car, I open the box and find a necklace with a tiny bird pendant inside. In a flash, a memory triggers: It's of Mom singing me to sleep when I was little. She'd always try for "Twinkle, Twinkle" or "Rock-a-Bye Baby," but I'd say, "No, sing 'Three Little Birdies.'"

"That's a silly one," she'd protest, embarrassed by her made-up song.

"It's the only one I like," I'd say. And eventually, always, she'd sing.

"Pretty," Sean says, about the necklace.

"Yeah, it is," I say, wiping away a tear before he sees. Betsey looks back at the necklace in my hands, then smiles.

"Like the song, right?" she asks.

"Like the song."

From the front seat, Betsey starts humming quietly. After all these years, after everything, I still remember the lyrics.

> Little birds, little birds in a line—count them:
> One, two, three!
> Painted blue, sitting on a vine—count: one, two, three!
> One eats worms; Two sings high; Three chases bees
> and butterflies.
> Little birds, little birds in a row; you look the same
> but you're not, oh,
> Fly, little birdies, fly.

Three Little Thank-Yous

One for my professional network. Dan and the rest of the Writers House gang (Cecilia, Chelsey, Stephen, and Torie), you are flat-out awesomesauce. Elizabeth, Jessica, JoAnna, Pam, and everyone at Little, Brown, I'm so happy to be part of the family. Ali at Egmont UK, Karri at Hardie Grant Egmont, and other editors worldwide, thank you for continuing to help deliver my books to a global audience. (See, Ali, Sean's not so bad, right?) Author, bookseller, librarian, and blogger buddies: I salute you.

One for those who helped make *The Originals* feel as real as possible. My science advisor, Janine, don't ever leave me. My music advisor, Jen, thank you for keeping me inspired. Mark, thank you for your last-minute input on small airports and charter planes.

And one for my family and friends. It takes a village, and mine rocks. Hubby, Monkeys, Mom, Dad, siblings, Grandpa, in-laws, extended family, neighbors, and dear friends near and far: Thank you for enthusiasm, humor, love, and support. At the time of this writing, there are two new family members cooking in bellies: I can't wait to meet you both. And to Kristin, who thinks that Lizzie B. is most like me. You might just be right.